Deuces Wild

By Jean Holloway

Published by PHE Ink
P. O. Box 940217
Houston, TX 77094

PHE Ink and the portrayal of the quill feather are trademarks of PHE Ink.

The cataloging-in-publication data is on file with the Library of Congress.

Library of Congress Control Number: 2010913290

ISBN: 978-1-935724-04-9 print; 978-1-935724-52-0 eBook

October 2010

Genre: Fiction/Thriller

Acknowledgment

To PHE Ink and my partner, TL James, you are more than a publisher. Under your guidance and protective wing, our authors: LM Blakely, T. Nicole, Otis Randolph, P. Renee, Jazz Singleton and I have become a literary family. And we all know how important family is to me.

Once again, I'd like to thank my advance readers and good friends, Shonna Peters, Sarah Yarborough and Bobbie Crawford-McCoy who encouraged me to stay true to my characters, no matter how uncomfortable it made me. Your input is priceless.

To the wonderful blog talk radio hosts and hostesses who have interviewed me over the years. Thanks for helping me reach readers who would not have heard of me otherwise.

To all the reviewers and book clubs who have supported me through the years, especially APOOO, Family Affair, Journey Thru Words, KC Girlfriends, OOSA, RAWSISTAZ, Readers In Motion, Savvy Sisters, Shades of Ebony, Sistahfriend, Sisters Sippin' Tea and WeReadItAll. If I forgot to mention anyone, remember, I'm 60!

And a special shout-out to all my literary sisters, but especially Trice Hickman, Gail McFarland and Marissa Monteilh. You make it a joy to be in this business.

Prologue

Thank God! It's Friday, was Lark McMillan's last thought before she snuggled under the covers next to her husband and dozed off. After a long, mentally exhausting week she slept soundly in their queen-size, waveless waterbed. A few hours later, she rolled to her left side and reached for Karl, only to find the sheets empty and cold. Alarmed, Lark instantly sat straight up, panting, unable to catch her breath. *Where is he?*

Her heart began to pound and she couldn't help but listen to the ominous thuds as they resonated loudly in her head. She lay perfectly still in the after-midnight darkness and took several deep breaths, forcing herself to calm her nerves. Looking down, she saw her fists tightly clutching the sheet and blanket. Lark slowly willed them to open and let go.

After the drum-like sound faded, she thought she heard a soft whisper. *Or was it more like a muffled groan?* She convinced herself that she heard the hushed sounds of stolen, illicit sex and then she knew *exactly* where he was.

She also knew she couldn't lay there and pretend it wasn't happening. She saw the stolen glances of lust and embarrassment between the two of them and tried to ignore it, but her suspicious nature told her she was playing the fool. She prayed that she would see nothing concrete to fuel her suspicions, but instinct told her that she had a right to be concerned...

When they met seven years ago, he seemed like a really nice guy - the answer to a single mother's prayer. It was early December and one day, after leaving work at the courthouse, she'd gone to *Toys R Us* to do a little early Christmas shopping for her eight-year-old daughter, Dahlia. She and Karl simultaneously reached for the last Strawberry Shortcake lunchbox on the shelf. She wanted it because Doll, as her daughter was affectionately called, resembled the illustration. Lark appreciated his chivalry when he graciously capitulated.

"Here, you take it. Looks like we have the same taste in toys for our little girls. I'll find something else for my niece. I'm Karl, with a 'K', McMillan," he introduced himself. She instantly recognized that even their names had symmetry.

Lark swiftly looked him up and down. He stood a shade under six feet; several inches taller than her five-foot-three with two-inch heels. But all in all, Karl was not a bad-looking guy. His receding hairline, coupled with his blond shoulder-length ponytail, said that he had a hint of rebel in him. His eyes were the darkest brown, almost black, but there was nothing ominous about them or his appearance. She offered to help him with finding a replacement toy for his niece. Together, they settled on the Cherries Jubilee edition of My Little Pony. Pleased with their gifts, they stood in the checkout line waiting to pay when he asked if she had enough time to have a drink with him. They went

to the phone booth outside the store so that she could check with her next-door neighbor, who watched her daughter when necessary. After her neighbor's approval, she was good to go. Drinks led to dinner and before she realized it, night had fallen. Always the gentleman, he walked her to the "L" and they exchanged numbers while waiting for her train. Lark hoped she would see him again. She thought about how great it would be to have a nice guy in her life.

After a slow start, they began dating exclusively. She wanted everything to be perfect, so unlike her occasional one night stands, she waited before giving herself to him. On their first night together, he pleased her in every way imaginable, making it well worth the wait. Four months later, in late May of 1978, Lark finally admitted to herself that she had fallen head over heels for the man. She brought him home to her tiny, one-bedroom apartment to meet her only child, Dahlia. She'd been a little hesitant at first because in the past, there were several men, like her parents, who believed raising a bi-racial child was not an ideal situation. If she listened to them, she would have given her daughter up for adoption long ago. *Hell, I may have even given her up at birth.*

Her parents never met their granddaughter's father and didn't care that he had been a decorated Vietnam War casualty. She didn't realize how racist they were until she'd shown up at their door with her baby. Her father refused to acknowledge the child at all and her mother... Well, she was a piece of work too.

"At least she doesn't look like a Negro!" Lark's mother joked, in poor taste, as she took the baby from her arms. She laid Doll on the plastic-covered, gold brocade couch and opened the pink blanket to take a peek at her grandchild. Without a word, Lark hastily bundled her

daughter up and left her parents' home. She hadn't spoken to either of them since. The last time she saw her mother was at her father's funeral and they acted like strangers and ignored each other through the entire service and burial. It hurt her deeply to see her sister and brother take her mother's side of the dispute. *Bunch of bigots,* she constantly thought throughout that long, dreary day.

Lark thought the situation was ironic, since one would have never known her child's lineage by looking at her. In fact, she had yet to share the secret with her daughter. Doll had her father's brown eyes, but she was a true redhead - freckles and all. She embodied the picture of innocence and could have easily won a starring role in a Disney movie. No one thought of her as Black unless Lark chose to divulge that information. It surprised her when she heard some of the Black folks on her block refer to her daughter as a "redbone". She never felt the need to mention it, yet somehow they could tell.

Life became a struggle for the two of them. Lark was entirely alone, since her mother continued to influence her siblings. She convinced them that having a child of mixed heritage disgraced the entire family. Lark took on the responsibility of caring for herself and her daughter with a fierceness she didn't know she possessed. And yes, sometimes, she had to do things that she wasn't particularly proud of to make ends meet. She needed money to finish paying for court reporting school and after graduation she needed funds to tide her over until she got a job with the state. When Lark and Doll were together, Lark had a tendency towards spoiling her daughter. She did it to help make up for the times she wasn't there and to compensate for the lack of family members present in Doll's life. Occasionally, on the way home from school or

work, she would stop and have one drink too many. Other times, she stayed out a little too late. But she always let whoever was watching Dahlia know in advance. Hell, life was short and she deserved to have some fun.

The first time she brought Karl home, she realized that all her worries were unfounded. She couldn't believe how quickly her daughter took to him and Lark could see the feeling was mutual. They had an instant, undeniable bond. It was almost as if they magically transformed into the family they all wanted to be. The three became inseparable.

When she finally broke down and told him about Doll's biological father, Karl said all the right things. He told her how proud he would be to help raise the daughter of a war veteran and that race didn't mean a thing. It solidified their relationship even more. He quickly moved them into his two-bedroom apartment on Bruckner Boulevard in the Bronx. When everyone felt at home and settled, he proposed to Lark on a beautiful summer evening in 1982. She happily accepted.

Later that year, Karl earned a promotion to district manager. He was the lead salesman for a pharmaceutical company for three years running and had been a shoo-in for the position, even over some of his co-workers with more seniority.

They were married the following year on a beautiful spring day in April and relocated to a charming, yellow-shingled Cape Cod on the southern tip of Portsborough. They were now the normal, middle-class American family.

Everything seemed so perfect until about six months ago. That's when Doll suddenly went from a sweet and gentle child to a moody pre-teen who carried a constant chip on her shoulder. Her freckles were fading and she

started wearing makeup to help cover the few that remained. Lately, the makeup seemed a little much for a young teenager. Lark told her to cut it out, washed her face and confiscated numerous cosmetics, yet less than a couple of weeks later, Doll managed to replenish her supply and defiantly began to wear it again. The big blowup came when Doll forgot her gym bag and Lark found the skimpy, sexy schoolgirl outfit at the bottom under her P.E. uniform.

Lark had been sitting on the bed, waiting in her room which now looked like a tornado had blown through it. Everything was everywhere; her daughter's open closet door revealed it was empty, a couple of the dresser drawers were on the floor and the others appeared to be hanging on for dear life. Totally covered with rumpled clothes, you couldn't see the soft green tweed carpet.

Doll walked in and ignored the obvious mess.

"Why are you in my room, Mom?"

"You left your gym bag and I looked inside. What the hell is this?" Lark stood up and held the tiny denim skirt and ruffled, shocking pink cotton midriff blouse in her left hand.

"A skirt and top?" Doll asked sarcastically.

Lark ceremoniously pulled the pinking shears from behind her back.

"Looks more like dust cloths to me." She commented as she began cutting the clothes into even smaller pieces.

None of this fazed Doll.

"Have fun, there's more where those came from. Now, I guess I have to clean my room. Do you mind?"

Before she knew what happened, Lark leaped across the

room and slapped Doll with all the strength she could muster. Horrified at her actions, Lark had been the one to run out of the room in tears.

Since then, Doll seemed to convey an undeserving disdain for Lark and she didn't even attempt to hide it. At first, Lark blamed it on puberty, but no matter how difficult it was to admit, she couldn't deny the truth any longer. She knew why Doll's attitude changed so radically. Her husband, Karl, was molesting her fifteen-year-old daughter.

Lark slowly moved over to his side of the queen-size bed and removed the black and gray 9mm Ruger P89DC from the maple nightstand's bottom drawer. The two pound pistol felt especially heavy in her hands tonight. She removed the magazine and after she checked to make sure it was fully loaded with copper-tipped brass bullets, she slipped it back into the empty chamber. Then she crept out of their bed.

Lark knew she was capable of killing him. Ironically, he was the one who had started taking her to the range for target practice. She ran her fingers over the smooth barrel and it evoked a memory so strong she could almost smell a whiff of burnt gunpowder. It all flooded back as his instructions replayed in her mind.

They put on their headphones and Karl centered himself directly behind her. His hands enclosed hers as he adjusted her grip. Lark felt him bend his knees into the backs of hers. Reflex made her fall into place against his body and she became aroused. Strangely, a man at her back and a gun in her hands felt like one of the most sensual moments of her life.

Now focus, inhale and pull the trigger as you exhale.

Her aim had gotten quite good. After only a few weeks of practice, she discovered she was quite the expert at head and neck shots.

Lark wrapped the pink terry cloth robe around her sturdy body, tying the belt while looking down on what used to be her waistline. At five feet one, one hundred and sixty-five pounds, she wished she could magically get her teenage body back. *Maybe then, he wouldn't have...* but she knew her figure had nothing to do with what was happening in the other bedroom. Although it wasn't her fault, her guilt made her feel otherwise. Her stomach churned.

Barefoot, she walked up the light beige carpeted stairs to her daughter's room on the right. Lark stopped, stood by the door and listened. When she thought she heard a soft moan, she quietly turned the knob, opened the door and flicked on the light switch. What happened next would haunt her in recurring flashbacks for the rest of her life.

Although Lark thought she knew what they were doing, she wasn't prepared for the sight of the two of them caught in the act. It didn't appear to be rape. It looked more like a couple enjoying the epitome of unbridled sex. This was worse than she could have ever imagined. Her little girl was riding her husband with wild abandon. Facing him on her knees, Doll was so into it that she looked like a contortionist. The phrase "bent over backward" came to mind as she watched her daughter's wavy, chestnut hair rhythmically brush across his legs. Karl's hands were gripping her hips so tightly that she could see the pale imprint of his fingers against her skin, guiding her movements. She noticed that his feet were fully extended so much so that they were parallel to the bed, his toes pointed. Lark knew that meant he was totally engrossed in

the joy of raw sex. She'd seen that sign before, except she had been the one on top. She watched as he rhythmically moved beneath her daughter, thrusting hard to reach deep inside her, oblivious that his actions were no longer a secret. The two were so lost in each other that it took them a moment to react to the light and acknowledge her presence.

Two pairs of eyes registered shock, but it was the third pair, her daughter's eyes, that made her feel even more uneasy. They contained no shame - but rather a smidgen of defiance. It resembled hate with a hint of triumph.

This had turned out far worse than her greatest fear. She hesitated, ashamed that for a split second, she was unsure of which one of them she should shoot. Karl stopped and violently pushed Doll onto the floor. Lark didn't know if it was an act of chivalry or humiliation, but with her daughter out of the way, she aimed. She heard the loud blast and inhaled a whiff of that familiar gunpowder smell.

"What the fuck, Mom? You could have at least waited 'til I came!" Doll yelled as she picked herself up.

The tone of Doll's voice shocked her as much as her words did. *What was she saying?* Lark tried to make sense of it all in her mind. She looked down at her hands and saw they were empty. The pistol had fallen to the floor.

"What?"

"You heard me. Now, look at the mess you've made."

"Wait...I shot him because...I thought he was raping you."

"Raping me?" Her daughter's extreme eye-rolling would have been comical in any other situation. "We've

been fucking for almost a year now, *Mom*." She said it so mockingly, Lark gasped. "If anything, I was raping him. Now, we need to get our story straight before the police get here."

"Why didn't you tell me?"

"I don't think that was on our agenda, sorry."

Doll picked up the Ruger, put it into Karl's hands and pressed his fingers all over the grip, trigger and barrel. Satisfied, she aimed at his groin and squeezed off another shot.

"Okay, so this is how it went...He raped me at gunpoint, I grabbed for the gun, we fought, somehow the gun went off and I accidently shot him in the head. I was so distraught and so angry that I shot him again in the groin. I didn't realize he was already dead and did it to make sure he'd never try to rape me again. You heard the shots, came in and this is how you found us. You snatched the gun from me. That'll explain all of our prints. Now all you have to do is call the police and make sure we keep the story straight. You think you can do that?"

"You...You want me to say you killed him?"

"*Yes*, Mom," she answered in an exasperated tone. It was as if Doll suddenly became the parent. "I'm a minor. The most they'll do to me is send me to Juvie 'til I'm eighteen, but you could go to prison for life. You wouldn't want that, would you?"

Still in shock, Lark slowly shook her head "no" and left to go back to her bedroom. Her hands trembled as she dialed '911'. At that precise moment, she realized two things; that her life would never be the same and that she didn't know her child at all.

But then again, no one really did.

Some people are natural born con artists. Doll's main agenda was always seeing how much she could get away with. After all, she considered herself smarter than the average bear. Yet, she never wondered whether or not anyone would believe her enough to let her do whatever she wanted. They always did. She considered herself slick - and she loved it. To Doll, life was like a puppet show and she was the master puppeteer. Her ultimate goal was to eventually let the world in on her secret.

Portsborough, NY 1989

Chapter One

THE PERSISTENT SOUND of the alarm clock interrupted one of her worst nightmares. Shevaughn jumped up and hit the buzzer, grateful for the timing. It took a moment to shake off her feeling of dread. She'd always heard that if you die in a dream that you would die in real life. The alarm woke her up just before her dream ended. She'd been experiencing a series of nightmares during the last couple of months.

The dream started out innocently enough. The five of them were on a road trip. They were riding in a brand new black Lincoln Continental with cream leather interior instead of their tan Mitsubishi van. Marcus was driving and she was riding shotgun. She, Marcus and Toni were singing "Be Thankful", one of her favorite Loose Ends jams, as it played on the radio. Shevaughn had just unhinged her seatbelt in order to turn and give the baby a bottle when she heard a loud pop. The car began to spin and the bottle flew out of her hand, hitting Toni on her forehead. She heard her daughter scream and Shevaughn was hurled against the windshield. Suddenly everything began to move in slow motion. The spinning stopped and the car began to slide backwards down a huge embankment. It didn't stop until the Lincoln descended

almost five hundred feet, reaching a creek at the bottom of the hill. They began to sink into the cold, dark water.

Shevaughn climbed over the front seat and reached for her terrified children whose eyes were wider than she'd ever seen them.   They were both screaming as Toni scrambled into the front of the car and grabbed for Marcus. Shevaughn fought to get the baby out of the car seat. The latch that kept him belted in was jammed and she watched in horror as the water rose over his head.

"God help us," she screamed and then mouthed the words 'I love you' to her family as the water rose over her lips and began to fill her nostrils. Thankfully, the alarm went off at that exact moment.

She thought she might have thrashed out during the nightmare and glanced at Marcus. Surprised to see her husband still sleeping peacefully, she kissed his cheek. When he smiled without opening his eyes, she knew everything was as it should be. They were fine. Relieved, she got up, took her shower and started a breakfast of cinnamon toast, eggs, sausage and coffee. Her dream reinforced how happy her life made her, but it also reminded her that tomorrow wasn't promised. That was one of the reasons why she worked so hard to make every day count.

After getting Marcus off to work and dropping Toni at school, she drove to the precinct. Walking inside, she realized that it looked nothing like it did two years before. It had finally come into the twentieth century. There was a Tandy 5000 computer on each desk with a matching Tandy dot matrix printer which took up almost half of the desk's surface. There were also changes that weren't readily

visible, like the new Motorola flip phone each detective now carried.

Yesterday they'd closed a case of a robbery gone wrong. It ended with the arrest of a sixteen-year old boy. They charged him with first degree murder. In his quest for fast money, he not only ended a storekeeper's life, but he also ended his own future.

She and Jared were discussing how one stupid decision could cause a person to throw the rest of their life away when her desk phone rang.

"Detective Williams, Homicide." After listening to the person on the line, she replied, "Yes, I know where that is. We'll be right there." She turned to her partner. "Jared, someone reported finding a body behind Eddie's Lounge. Let's go."

Detective Shevaughn Williams looked up and down both sides of the street in front of the club before she continued down the alley. She walked inside the perimeter of the yellow tape barrier which designated the crime scene. A half dozen fellow officers were taking photos and dusting for fingerprints at the rear of Eddie's Lounge, a neighborhood club whose clientele mainly consisted of the twenty-one to thirty crowd.

"Who called this in?" Shevaughn asked the patrolman next to her.

He pointed to a medium height, stocky man leaning against the red brick wall across the alley from the dumpster. An older Black man, yet still quite muscular, he looked like he may have been a boxer in his younger days, but now his gray hair and slight paunch were evidence that

it had been a long time since he'd been in the ring. Right now, he looked as if he could have been knocked out by a breeze. She walked over to the visibly shaken man.

"Sir, I'm Detective Williams and your name is?

"Bob, Bob Hill."

"Mr. Hill, would you mind if I ask you a few questions?"

"I already told everything I know to the other cop," he informed her. She could tell he was making an effort to control his emotions. He closed his eyes for a moment and pulled himself together. "But if you think it will help," he said and reconsidered her request. He began his story once again.

"I was sweeping down the alley, cleaning up all the cigarette butts dumped back here from last night before getting ready to open the club. I always like to start the day with a clean slate."

He must have realized he was getting side-tracked because he stopped, cleared his throat and went on with his story.

"I see this sneaker by the dumpster, right? At first, I'm thinkin' someone tossed it and missed the bin, so I walk over to get rid of it myself. I get closer and notice something's funny, like it doesn't look right 'cause it's not lying flat on the asphalt, you know, it's…at an angle. That's when I got the chills, but I still went in for a closer look. I see a leg, realize it's a body and I couldn't stop myself from looking further up at the face…well…at least where the face was supposed to be. But instead there's this flat, bloody grocery bag with pieces of the bone sticking out. I lost my breakfast. Someone beat the shit out of him, if

you'll pardon my French ma'am and I'm only saying 'him' because of the men's clothes. I got myself together and dialed '911'. And here we are."

"Is that your white '85 Camaro Z28 parked on the street?" She jotted notes in her new field notepad, a birthday gift from Marcus last October. For the last couple of years, all October meant to Shevaughn was that she had to get ready for Halloween, which Toni considered to be one of her favorite holidays.

"Yes, ma'am."

"Thank you Mr. Hill. After you give my officer your contact information, you're free to go. Take my card in case you think of anything."

Assuming the victim was murdered there, she wondered if that meant he used public transportation or had he walked to the club? *Maybe this was just the drop off point and had no bearing on where he died,* Shevaughn pondered and went to take a look for herself. As she walked toward the bin, she prayed she wouldn't be able to imagine the condition of the victim's face. She steeled herself against any sudden reaction and walked over to the body.

Considering the obvious destruction, she noted that the victim's clothes were unusually clean, except for the ten small bloody smudges on the khaki pants that had been made by the missing fingertips. *They dressed and dumped him,* Shevaughn surmised. It looked like, after encasing the head in a Pathmark bag, someone had taken to it with a fast ax. Mr. Hill was right. The skull was beaten so badly that it appeared to be only a couple of inches thick. She saw the bone shards sticking up through the blood-stained plastic bag and felt the individual hairs on the back of her

neck rise up. She got an ominous premonition of pure evil and then nature took over. Shevaughn had just enough time to turn away and walk a few steps before she tasted the vomit that collected at the back of her throat. When she tried to swallow, her stomach propelled her breakfast. Although it was a cool October morning, she broke out in a sweat. It took every ounce of her fortitude not to pass out.

The next thing she knew, Jared was beside her, grabbing her elbow and holding her up.

"You okay? Here, take this tissue. You want to sit down? Should I call Marc?"

"I'm fine. It just knocked the wind out of me, that's all."

Her stomach turned sour and she couldn't get the sight out of her mind. *Good Lord, just when you think you've seen it all!*

Jared walked Shevaughn back to their police car and made her sit on the passenger side. He turned the air on, directing the vents so that the breeze blew towards her face. It cooled her down without making her feel any better.

"Thanks, man. I'm okay," she lied. He was turning more and more into a mother hen. Sometimes it was cute, but right now it grated her nerves.

"Are you sure? I don't want my wife or brother-in-law mad at me."

It's funny how life sometimes throws a curve. Last month, when Jared and Kennedy married, they'd become one big happy family. Shevaughn hadn't realized how much she was missing until she found it with them. Her in-laws were terrific, except for spoiling Toni every chance they got. They hadn't had a little girl in the family since

Kennedy and you could tell they missed it. Their family was a testament to good morals and values. She thanked God that He'd seen fit to allow her to become a member. Shevaughn stood proud with the rest of them at Kennedy's law school graduation. When she was appointed as one of the assistant district attorneys for the New York Trials Division, the whole family celebrated with a trip to the Poconos. Shevaughn bonded with all of them over that long weekend. She loved her relatives almost as much as she loved her husband. Suddenly a peaceful and blessed feeling rushed over her and melted her irritation. He was just being kin.

"You're safe Jared. I'll tell them both you had my back."

"It's the front I'm worried about," he said as he looked her over. Jared changed the subject. "What do you think happened here? Looks like a whole lotta hate."

"Or anger. Was there any ID on the victim?"

"There's no wallet, so all we know is that it's a young man, possibly twenty-five to thirty, Asian or Hispanic, although it's hard to tell without a face. Dr. Spencer's on his way. Hopefully, he can put the pieces together and give us some answers."

"This doesn't look random to me. Someone purposely obliterated his identity. He wasn't killed here either - not enough blood splatter. Then the killer dressed and dropped him here after they crushed his skull and removed his fingertips. Did you notice how clean his clothes were?"

"Uh, yeah, and considering the condition of skull, someone was very careful about keeping the clothes clean. They must have cut off his fingertips last and bound them to keep them from bleeding. Otherwise there would be

blood inside the sleeves."

"You're right. Someone used duct tape to cover the amputated fingertips. Mind if I make a suggestion, Von?"

"Course not, what?

"If you want me to, I can take lead on this one," Jared volunteered.

So today was the day she would pass the torch, if only temporarily. She had accepted the inevitable weeks ago.

"Fine, be sure they collect the dumpster's contents and find out when the last pickup was, on GP. I don't want anything overlooked and I understand how someone could get sidetracked. We may be looking at a robbery-homicide since the victim's wallet is missing. We have to go through everything; from the club patrons as possible witnesses to taxi pickups and drop-offs, phone calls to and from the club for the last twenty-four hours; the works.

"Ask Dr. Spencer if they can reconstruct the skull, if not, dental records won't be much help. See if we can somehow get a print, maybe off his belt. Hopefully we'll come up with a something we can use to ID him. Find out if there are any security cameras in the vicinity that were pointed anywhere near this section of the alley. Fingerprinting the entire alley is a bit much right now since it's a public place, but I want the dumpster and its contents tested for prints. The perpetrator may have touched something when he dumped the body. Have I missed anything?"

"Nothing I can think of, but if something else comes up, I'll let you know."

"Yeah, I want to be kept in the loop."

Trusting that the investigation was in Jared's capable

hands she realized she was already late for her appointment and hastily left the crime scene.

Fidgeting in the wood-trimmed, cushioned, indigo blue pleather chair, Shevaughn waited for the receptionist to call her name. She couldn't get comfortable and knew she'd have an even harder time standing when it was her turn. She tried to concentrate on the Family Circle magazine she'd picked up from the wooden coffee table in the middle of the room, but the words blurred together as she felt another flutter. Well, it was more like a roll than a flutter. She tried to slouch down a little and cross her feet, but nothing seemed to help. It was all just a part of being almost eight months pregnant.

She attempted to think about anything else to take her mind off of her discomfort and concentrate on the future, but the image of the poor man in the alley kept getting in her mind's way. Anyone would think that all the years she spent as a detective would have desensitized her. She wished that it had. The memory of the gory sight remained with her and she had a hard time focusing on anything else. Besides, if it didn't bother her, she'd be ready to turn in her badge and gun.

Determined to change her thoughts, she refocused on counting her blessings. She loved her husband madly and Toni was growing up to be a little firecracker who constantly kept them all on their toes. Marcus insisted on formally adopting her and Shevaughn believed Tony would have given his approval. Now she couldn't wait to add another member to their family and give birth to their son.

For the last couple of years, she and Marcus began to

worry if it would ever happen. Shevaughn got on a health kick, going to the gym three times a week and eating right. After six months, she was in better shape than she'd been in years. Just when they finally decided that although it was very important, it wouldn't interfere with their happiness, they were blessed. *And now look at us, a family of four, well...almost. Just one more month to go,* she smiled to herself.

Tomorrow she would start maternity leave. Even though she felt confident in handing Jared this latest case, it bothered her that he might have to solve this one without her. The timing sucked. Until today, the crime rate had drastically declined, especially homicide cases. Portsborough seemed to be turning into a model metropolitan area. For a while, she thought she wouldn't have a hard time letting go, but now? Shevaughn tried to refocus again. *Let it go...*

She sighed and listened to her soul, the same way she did when she complied with Dr. Herron's recommendation that she take the last month of her pregnancy off. Besides, Marcus insisted she follow the doctor's advice and she would have argued, except secretly she believed they were both right. She was close enough to forty to make everyone a little nervous. *Well, so far so good, thank God.*

She knew Marcus wanted a boy and although Shevaughn would have preferred not knowing, he'd gone with her to the last appointment and together they found out they were having a son. Even Toni was excited about the baby and promised to be "the bestest big sister ever". Shevaughn had to admit that Toni had stepped up and proved her level of responsibility while caring for Kayla. She did everything for her dog; walked her (although she wasn't allowed to do it alone), fed her and even helped

bathe and brush her whenever necessary. Dressing her up was Toni's favorite activity, especially when they wore matching outfits. Shevaughn smiled as she imagined future family pictures.

Mattie, her close friend for the last two years, burst into the waiting room like a tornado, reminiscent of the first day she'd come into Shevaughn's life. There was something about Mattie that made people feel secure in her presence. She gave the instant impression that there wasn't anything she couldn't handle.

"What's up, Lil' Mama? I'm so sorry, Hon, I had client walk in at the last minute with two legal file storage boxes full of receipts. He wants me to do his taxes for the last two years. I had to have a lengthy consultation with him before I could leave. How ya feelin'?"

"Lil' Mama is pretty far from the truth. Right now I feel more like Jabba the Hut," Shevaughn admitted.

"Well, at least you're a cuter version."

"Gee, thanks, I guess…"

The day she met Mattie Austin, Shevaughn hadn't started out looking for a friend. She stopped by Portsborough Elementary to pick Toni up from her first day of second grade. When she got to the class, she saw her daughter engaged in conversation with a lean boy who appeared inches taller than the rest of the children. Something about Toni's demeanor made Shevaughn stop and watch. Toni's body language told her that her daughter's interest was more in the boy than in what he was saying. Convinced that she was watching her daughter experience her first crush, Shevaughn walked toward them

and checked out his first day of school outfit. In his starched pale blue and white-striped button-down short-sleeve dress shirt and creased khakis, his profile looked like that of a Harvard candidate. He turned his head and completed the picture with a pair of oversized tortoise-shell glasses. He looked like a young Black version of Clark Kent.

Shevaughn watched as Toni looked up into the boy's face; her crooked smile lighting up her eyes. She stood with her index finger in her mouth, her shoulders slowly shifting from side to side. Shevaughn recognized the signs. Her seven-year-old daughter was flirting! Shevaughn's brow wrinkled. Lord knows she wasn't ready for this. Someone brushed past her.

"Boy, didn't I tell you to stay in your class 'til I picked you up? You scared Ms. Patterson half to death when we realized you weren't there."

Before he could answer, she took him by the ear and began to lead him away. Shevaughn saw the disappointed look on Toni's face and spoke up.

"Hi," she said extending her hand. "I'm Von Williams and this is my daughter, Toni."

"I'm sorry, sometimes this boy..." She punctuated her sentence with a stern look in his direction. Shevaughn noticed the boy returned the look and didn't flinch. Something told her he saw it as being macho in front of his girl. *So the feeling is mutual.*

"Hi, I'm Mattie Austin and this is my son, Quincy. Everyone just calls him Q. You know, you look so familiar to me. Have we met?"

"I doubt it, but you may have seen me on the news."

Mattie's eyebrows rose.

"It's a long story and I need to get home in time to start dinner."

"Girl, you can't drop a bomb like that and leave me hangin'. Think you'll have time to tell me the story after work Friday? I can leave Quincy with his dad. Think hubby would mind if we have a girls' night out? You pick the place."

"Well, I...Sure, why not? Marc wouldn't mind. How 'bout we meet at that club on Marlboro, you know, The Speakeasy? I hear they make a slammin' Fuzzy Navel."

Since then, they were as inseparable as any two working mothers could be. Sometimes, they just went over each others' house, drank wine and talked, but when Shevaughn found out the Austins played Bid Whist, well, they too became extended family. Shevaughn could tell Toni was delighted when they visited, since they always brought Quincy with them. Two grades ahead of Toni, he became her self-appointed tutor. Shevaughn knew Toni was happy with whatever brought him into close proximity and her grades actually improved. She was keeping a close eye on those two.

"I heard about the body they found near the dumpster downtown."

The events of the morning rushed back and all of Shevaughn's blessings seemed to fade away.

Chapter Two

DOLL HENDERSON STILL thought back to the day her mom killed her stepdad. *Didn't think the old bat had it in her!* Everything went almost exactly as she predicted, especially once the police found evidence of her stepfather's sperm inside her, but the groin shot made self defense a hard story for the jury to swallow. The big surprise came when they sentenced her to Juvenile Hall until she turned twenty-one, not eighteen, due to the severity of the second degree murder charge. The judge gave her double the time she expected. It would have been a long six years in Juvie, especially since she thought she would only serve three, yet Doll looked at the whole experience as a dress rehearsal. Her uniform was her costume. She entered Juvie as an apprentice manipulator and used the time to hone her skills. The psychologist said she suffered from nymphomania which made her an easy target. She never thought of herself as prey. If people saw her that way it meant she'd gotten over on all of them, especially since no one knew her secrets. They were secrets that she would never tell anyone because if she did, no one would ever think of her as prey again...

Doll's road to Hell began during her twelfth summer. The year had been a hard one for her. She'd tested to get into an accelerated school. When the results came back,

they called Lark and offered Doll a full scholarship to attend their prestigious school. Excited, Lark told her daughter the news. She couldn't believe it. The school told her that they were excited to have her. Everything went as planned until the school did a background check and discovered that her pedigree wasn't up to their standards. Suddenly, they were so sorry. An unexpected loss of funds prevented them from being able to provide the scholarship. Doll wanted her mother to sue, but instead, Lark decided to send Doll to stay with her godmother in Philly for two weeks as if it were a consolation prize. Hurt, Doll began packing her things a week early. After she got over the fact that she had been denied admittance because of the Black father she never knew, Doll chose to ignore how much it hurt and make the best of things.

This was the first time she was leaving home and Aunt Morgan fascinated her since Doll realized Morgan was the only lesbian she'd ever met. She was in awe of a woman so sure of herself and her sexuality that she didn't conform to the standard and was proud of it, aside from how good she looked in the tailored men's clothes she occasionally wore. It had taken her a while to figure it out since she was too young to think about what people did behind closed doors until one day she was sitting on the floor watching TV. Doll changed channels until an old ABC movie caught her attention. *Question of Love* told the story of a lesbian trying to keep her baby after a divorce. One of the leading actresses said something and immediately Aunt Morgan came to mind. That's when Doll started putting two and two together.

Her mom rode the train with her from New York and Aunt Morgan was waiting for them at the Philly station. She closely watched the two women greet each other,

hoping to see if she could spot something that would tell her their friendship was more than just that. Doll was disappointed when she couldn't see anything out of the ordinary. They hugged, talked a bit and hugged some more. Lark kissed her daughter, told her to behave and then Aunt Morgan took her home in her first ride in a cab. Doll whispered, "Wow," as they pulled up in front of the cool brownstone. It even had a green postage-size lawn and a small red maple tree. *Aunt Morgan must be rich!* There was more graffiti than grass outside their little, rent-controlled, city apartment. *This looks like something out of a magazine!* She followed her godmother down the hall to the stairway, her eyes darting from side to side, taking in the art displayed on the walls. She'd never seen Black art before. At the top of the stairs, there was a small bathroom and then they turned right and Aunt Morgan showed her the room that belonged to her for the next fourteen days. She couldn't believe it. It was pink and there was a queen-size canopy bed with a matching dresser and night tables. With pastel pictures of Black women in gardens, by a swing, or at tea, the room had an air of fantasy and looked fit for a princess. Waking up in the beautiful room the next morning, she loved the bay window that let in the sunlight. It even had a window seat that she hadn't noticed the night before. Doll stretched, feeling better than she ever remembered feeling before.

The bliss was short-lived. Boredom set in by the fourth day. It wasn't easy playing little Miss Goody Two-Shoes twenty-four hours a day. There didn't seem to be anything exciting to do. After a lunch of tuna fish sandwiches, potato chips and fresh lemonade, her godmother left her with a jigsaw puzzle as if she had the patience for something so stupid. Doll moved pieces around for a half hour and then

went to find her.

"Aunt Morgan, do you know any kids my age?"

"Not really, child. I thought we'd go to the library in a little bit, get you some books. Do you have any favorites?"

Books! She's gotta be kidding me. This is gonna be a long two weeks.

"Wait, you know, I do have a friend that has a boy about your age. I'll give her a call."

She watched Aunt Morgan call her friend, doubting that any boy her age would want to be bothered with her and couldn't believe her ears when she heard her say, "Okay, just have him drop by tomorrow, say around ten?" Doll stood dumbfounded and waited until her godmother hung up the phone.

"He's coming?"

"Yes, said he'd love to meet you, I've talked about you so much."

Doll wondered what she could have possibly said to make a boy want to meet her, but it was hard to think with her heart beating so rapidly and loud. She went to her room and started going through her clothes, trying to find something appropriate for this important meeting. After dinner, she excused herself early claiming she was tired, but it was really because she knew the sooner she got to sleep, the sooner tomorrow would come.

That night she had a fairy tale dream of a handsome prince coming to rescue her from this summer vacation hell. She woke up in a great mood. After showering, brushing her teeth and dressing, Doll came downstairs to the smell of bacon and maple syrup. Aunt Morgan had

made pancakes. It took all her resolve to eat a couple of them without vomiting. Her nerves were making her nauseous and eating slowly only made it worse. Then it finally turned ten o'clock and she heard the doorbell ring. She sat in the living room in her short brown and pink floral sundress. Doll considered it her most provocative outfit because it was so short.

When he entered the room, she felt immediate disappointment. He wasn't even close to the handsome prince she imagined. Short and stocky, he looked more like a troll from one of Grimm's fairy tales. When he smiled, he displayed yellow buck teeth. He wore an old wax print African safari shirt and khaki pants with black leather Adidas that had seen better days. He got near enough to take her hand during the introduction and she got a close-up of his nasty face. Doll almost gagged from the stench of his breath. Her vacation had just gotten longer. Aunt Morgan made the introduction. *Who the hell looks at a baby and names him Wilbur?* She fought an urge to shake her head, doing her best Mr. Ed imitation. She'd watched the show on Nick at Nite during a free cable weekend. *Maybe he's got horse breath.* She snorted and covered it up by pretending to sneeze. They sat in the parlor in uncomfortable silence, both looking down to avoid staring at each other.

He cleared his throat and asked, "How old are you?"

"Thirteen," she lied. "How old are you?"

"Fourteen, I'll be fifteen the end of next month."

Ahh, an older man...

"Wanna go to the movies?"

At least then we won't need conversation.

"Sure, I've been dying to see *Dead Calm*, but..." She was going to say "my mom wouldn't let me" and decided against it. It sounded childish. "Okay, let's ask if we can go."

Aunt Morgan was glad to let them go. She gave Doll a five-dollar bill for admittance and snacks.

When the movie got to the part where Billy Zane tried to get to Nicole Kidman by battering down the door, he reached over and took her hand. She closed her eyes and once again pretended he was the handsome prince she'd dreamed of. Wilbur surprised her by letting her hand go and then lightly brushed his fingers against her budding breasts. Doll felt her one of her first twinges of lust. Even though he didn't appeal to her, it still felt good.

He slipped his hand under her short skirt and found the space between her and her panties, sending a shock throughout her body. She sat in silence as he began to concentrate on the center of her newborn sexuality. He flicked his finger back and forth until she was on the edge of an orgasm and then stopped. She watched as he put the same finger in his mouth and sucked on it, his tongue circling his finger. Then he touched her with his moist fingertip and brought her to her first climax. He went back to watching the movie until the credits ran. Doll had no idea how the film ended.

On the way home, they stopped in an alley behind Woolworth's and he let her touch him. She was fascinated with his smooth, sturdy penis and gave him her first hand job.

Wilbur visited with her almost every day after their first "date". Whenever they had a stolen moment, they would touch, although he never attempted penetration. Aunt

Morgan seemed unaware of what they were up to...until the night they took it too far.

A faint sound from across the room woke Doll. She ignored it at first, but the persistent tapping on the window won out and she went to see what caused it. Wilbur stood under her window, throwing rocks.

"Can I come up?"

"I don't know, can you?"

"Watch me," he countered as he put his foot on the lower window ledge and hoisted himself up. It was like watching a slug crawl vertically, but the twinge between her legs came back all the same. She reached out, grabbed his hands and helped him in.

"Lay down," he said in a commanding voice. "Open your legs."

She did as told and he buried his face between them.

No wonder his breath stinks! Yet, she appreciated the way he made her feel. It was so intense that neither one of them heard Aunt Morgan open the door.

"Get the hell up!" She screamed brandishing a bat as she ran into the room. The two of them scurried like mice out of the bed and stood in front of it while trying to cover themselves. All three were aware of Wilbur's erection.

"Boy, we're calling your momma right now. Do you know I could have you arrested?"

♣♣♣

His hard-on began at the sound of the first rock hitting the glass. He didn't believe he was actually going through with it, but sex was all he thought of since the moment he

met her. She was so young, so innocent. She had no idea that he was a virgin. Girls weren't exactly throwing themselves at him. In fact, he always seemed to be the brunt of fat and ugly jokes. They usually snickered when he came into their line of vision. He'd only seen pictures of naked women in the magazines he found hidden in the brown wicker hamper in his parents' bathroom.

By the time she opened the window, his erection was full-blown, pun intended, considering that was all he'd thought about for the last four hours. It was hard to climb up to her window due to his weight and because he couldn't help but focus on the throbbing. It was painful, but in a good way. As soon as his feet hit the floor, he began snatching off his clothes, eager to release the monster he'd become. Convinced he had the largest penis on the planet, he was eager to try it out, but remembered reading somewhere that she was supposed to be wet. He decided to taste her before letting her touch him, thus prolonging the moment. Wilbur buried his face in her lap and had just felt her flesh on the tip of his tongue when all hell broke loose.

The rest of the night flew by like snowflakes in a blustery storm. Wilbur's mother came, apologized profusely to them both and proceeded to smack him around for what seemed like hours. On the way out, they all heard her say, "Wait 'til your father hears about this." Then Aunt Morgan made the dreaded phone call to her mother.

The next thing she knew, she was packed and on a train home the following night. The ninety-minute ride was torture. She kept imagining her mother waiting at the

station with the entire police force. Surely they could get arrested for what they did. She could almost feel the handcuffs around her wrists. Doll stepped off the train and saw her mother walking towards her, alone and crying. *What the…?*

"My baby, my poor baby, you don't need to say anything. Aunt Morgan told me all about what that nasty boy tried to do to you. I should have never let you go. I'm so sorry. Can you forgive me?"

A powerful emotion swept through her body as she realized what her mother's words meant. *I'm not in trouble! I got away with it!* Tears formed and suddenly she was crying as hard as her mother, except hers were tears of relief.

Chapter Three

FOR THE REST of the summer, Doll used shoplifting and masturbation to satisfy her needs. Shoplifting gave her the thrill she needed and she got a rush every time she left a store without that dreaded tap on her shoulder. She got rather good at it, but had to hide most of the things she acquired. To her, not being found out added to the fun. After a month or so, she needed to go on to bigger and better things for gratification. Besides, things began to accumulate and she knew it wouldn't be long before her mom found them and demanded an explanation. She began to think of other ways to get the same exhilaration.

One day, Lark sent her to pick up a few things for dinner and a stranger stopped her in the produce section of the A & P. As she watched the good-looking boy dressed in torn acid-washed jeans and a t-shirt come towards her, she found she couldn't move. His resemblance to the prince she'd dreamed of was remarkable. He casually asked her what she did for fun. She couldn't remember what she said and was totally taken by surprise when he asked for her phone number. *He's flirting with me!* With no hesitation, she rattled off her number and then became nauseated when she realized how much trouble she would be in if he called and her mom answered the phone. Every time the phone rang, her stomach would flip with excitement. It

was the same thrill she'd gotten in Grand Central. The thought that he had looked at her as a woman and not as a little girl surprised and pleased her.

The following week, she tried to catch the phone on the first ring as if it were a matter of life and death, but after he hadn't called for several days, she got lax and forgot about it until one evening she heard her mom scream, "Boy, do you know how old she is? Call here again and I'll have you arrested". Months later, she would still get sick with anticipation every time her mom sent her to the store, hoping she would run into him again. She never did.

At thirteen, she got her first babysitting job. Her mother thought it would be a good idea for her to start making her own money. She talked to one of her churchgoing friends and convinced her to let Doll babysit their ten-month-old son while she and her husband went out for dinner and a movie. They left Doll with instructions and phone numbers and went about their merry way. She slowly walked around their beautiful home pretending it belonged to her. She especially liked the immaculate modern kitchen with its matching avocado green appliances. Doll opened the fridge and discovered that they had stocked it with sodas and all kinds of luncheon meat. They'd even thought to stock the freezer with frozen pizzas in case she got hungry.

During her tour, she'd found their liquor cabinet and poured herself a drink. There were bottles of bourbon, scotch, vodka and rum. Doll took a little from each of the open bottles, hoping no one would notice. She added ice and a splash of cola.

Taking her concoction to the living room, she turned on the TV and sank into the comfortable rust-colored corduroy recliner. She sipped her drink and was just getting into

idiot mother.

Weak from the experience, she got up, slowly put back on her pants and dressed the baby in a clean diaper and cute little tan bunny pajamas. Doll took him to the kitchen, heated one of his bottles and went back to the recliner. There, she fed him while softly singing "Summertime" in a surprisingly good *mezzo-soprano* voice. It wasn't long before she watched his eyes become heavy and he stopped sucking. She kissed Teddy on his forehead and laid him in his crib. He grabbed a small stuffed dog that was in the center of the crib and put his thumb in his mouth. Watching him, she got a wet, gripping sensation in what she now considered to be the most important part of her body. She closed her eyes and swayed while enjoying the feeling.

She got herself together and took the nasty clothes and sheets downstairs to the garage, put them in the washing machine, started the load and came up to finish her drink. When it was gone, she went back into the bathroom and used what she assumed was the mother's toothbrush since it was pink, brushed her teeth and gargled with Listerine.

Mr. and Mrs. Blake came home a little after eleven. They praised her for taking such good care of their son and going the extra mile by washing the dirty laundry. The father paid her and took her home. No one, except her, was the wiser. She knew she was safe when the Blakes started recommending her to other parents. Soon, she had babysitting gigs every Friday and Saturday night. Not once did they suspect why she showed a preference for babysitting little boys younger than a year old. Everyone trusted her to watch their kids and it assured her that they had no idea.

That's why it was so easy for her to con the staff into thinking what she wanted them to think, that she was the poor little victim. Her tiny five-foot, ninety-pound stature and innocent demeanor made everyone want to take care of her. They all wished the best for her and she used it to her fullest advantage. By the time she was released, the staff and most of the other inmates loved her. Contrary to the verdict, no one believed she could have committed murder unless she acted in self defense.

Chapter Four

THE ONE PERSON most concerned with Doll's well-being was Reuben Mendoza, a quiet, eighteen-year-old Puerto Rican-Cubano boy she'd met last year in group therapy. Once every other week, groups from the separate juvenile halls met with a psychologist. Right before their visits, there was always sexual tension in the air since the only other males the girls got to see were the guards. She'd lucked out when he became a member of her group. His dark good looks caught her attention the first time he entered the group therapy room. At 5'11", he resembled a taller, darker version of Andy Garcia, the young actor, except he had a cuter nose and his body was cut due to all his time in the Juvie gym. She realized he wasn't what she considered fine, yet there was an edge about him, a *really* sexy edge. He couldn't have been more to her liking if she had created him herself. The first time she looked into his eyes and then at his crotch, she felt a familiarity. It felt like their bodies and souls knew each other from a prior life and the realization hit her like a bolt of lightning.

♣♣♣

Reuben came to Juvie for the attempted murder of Miguel, his mom's boyfriend. That day two years ago, school let out early due to some teacher's meeting. He'd gotten home early, excited over the anticipation of

spending some time alone without Miguel, his sister or his mom invading his space. When he walked into the living room of the small house, he was shocked to see Miguel and some woman he didn't recognize laying together on the couch. He could smell alcohol and sex in the air. Miguel shooed the woman out of the house in a hurry and warned Reuben not to say a word about any of it to his mom.

After a dinner filled with tense silence, Miguel slid his chair away from the card table they now used for meals since he'd broken the dining table in their last fight.

"I'm going out for a while," Miguel announced.

"Where?" His mother timidly asked.

Reuben heard her voice shake. He had witnessed this scene a hundred times. Sometimes, he hated her for being such a weakling. She never stood up for herself.

"Are you questioning me?" Miguel asked in a threatening tone.

"I just thought, maybe you'd like some company."

"I said I, not we. I'm hanging with the boys. And don't bother waiting up."

Miguel grabbed his bomber jacket and left the apartment.

While he was gone, Reuben told his mother what he witnessed. Enraged, she waited for him and when he got home, the argument turned into a physical fight. Miguel smacked them both around, her for questioning him and him for telling. After backhanding his mom into the kitchen wall, Miguel stood over her, ranting, his fists balled up at his side. He was so drunk and enraged that he didn't see Reuben grab a knife from the sink. Without considering

the consequences, Reuben lunged and stabbed Miguel in the chest, right under his shoulder blade, missing his heart by inches. Convicted of stabbing his mother's boyfriend during a fight, he too, was incarcerated until the age of twenty-one. Because of the extenuating circumstances and the fact that the supposed "victim" fully recovered, the judge ordered probation with the stipulation that he receive extensive therapy.

Once Doll heard of his crime, she knew that he considered himself to be a protector of women. She not only became his woman, but she also became his purpose. Up until then her only sexual encounters, after her stepdad's, were her secret experimentations with some of the more passive girls in Juvie. It helped relieve the pressure. When Doll and Reuben found each other, she tossed "her woman" aside, which led to a nasty fight. Her actions landed her in solitary for ten days. Once she went back to her room, Doll slipped out of bed after lights out. She found her ex-partner and woke her up by putting her hand over her mouth. She'd made a shiv from wearing down the sides of a toothbrush on the concrete block wall of her cell. Now, she held it to the girl's throat, putting pressure on the carotid artery.

"If you ever try to touch me again, I swear you'll wake up too late. From now on, I'm 'strictly dickly', you got that?"

Obviously, she did because there were no more reconciliation attempts. The general populace knew Doll and Reuben were officially a couple after that night. They managed to sneak in a few moments together whenever they could. Because the sessions alternated between the

boys' and girls' juvenile halls, the two decided that when they were in the boys' hall, they'd meet in the girls' bathroom and vice versa. Doll and Reuben would go into their respective bathrooms first to make sure they were unoccupied. A couple of times, they did it in the chapel's confessional. There was no time for romance or foreplay and sometimes there was only enough time for a speedy blow job, but they took care of each other every way they could. She was always the aggressor.

During her incarceration, Doll became fascinated with true crime stories. It all started when she found out about the Black Dahlia case, one of Hollywood's most infamous unsolved murders. She never really cared for her name until she realized she shared it with the poor, bloodless corpse police found literally cut in half. It seemed like not only the perfect murder, but one of the strangest in history. Doll proudly considered herself the real Black Dahlia and starting using Henderson, her biological father's last name.

She began reading everything she could get her hands on connected with the murder. Starting with local stories, she learned about the two infamous serial murderers that originated in Portsborough and became familiar with all the details. She then branched out, looking for others in magazines, novels and even comic books. Doll wanted to know what the killers did wrong. Something told her that these facts would come in handy one day. She would take the cases and dissect them, putting her perspective on them, imagining herself as the killer and trying to learn from other murderers' mistakes. She played it like a game, getting very good at it with practice. *America's Most Wanted* became her favorite television show.

Reuben was released several months later and started outpatient therapy. That ended their physical contact. He

began to write her the sexiest love letters; telling her in detail what he would do to her the next time they were together. She thought of them as her masturbation letters and they kept her company while she waited for her release. The day finally came when she walked out of the metal, solid gray double doors for the last time. She couldn't wait to see him again. The thought brought such a rush of moisture that she wondered if she would have to change her panties.

Lark picked her up just outside the gates, her conversation full of plans for Doll's future. She tolerated her mom's endless chatter, her mind on Reuben. Her mother yapped on and on, talking about how lucky they were to get a new start.

As soon as they got home, back to where it all began, she felt stifled. She phoned him and slipped out of the house less than an hour later without letting Lark know. He was outside waiting for her in a 1970 pine green Chevy pickup. He drove a couple of miles from her home, pulled off the freeway and headed down a deserted access road. They made long-awaited love right there in the bed of his truck. Reuben then drove them to his studio apartment near the industrial park where they stayed in bed until the following afternoon.

Doll celebrated her first week of real freedom with several bottles of Gordon's vodka, a half ounce of weed that Reuben had waiting for her and sex any way and anywhere possible. When they wore each other out, he dropped her back at her mom's house, just in time for her to leave and make her weekly appointment with the probation officer. As they drove up to the house, Lark stood at the front door with a look of disapproval and Doll fluffed it off, ignoring her mother and giving all her

attention to Reuben. Holding her close, he promised to return the next weekend after work.

It only took her a couple of days to realize she couldn't stay under the same roof with that woman. Lark kept trying to contain and control her with her little girl talks and stupid plans. So when he finally came back, she swiftly moved her few things into his studio, paying no attention to Lark's protests. She was grown now and refused to be told what to do. *This is my time.*

Reuben constantly complained about how much he hated his boring, low-paying job. This didn't put him in a much of a partying mood, so Doll spent most of her time trying to coax him to come to the club with her. *After all, isn't that what being young means?* Then, one night, she realized she had a lot more fun without him and stopped pushing the issue. She felt no guilt about leaving him home alone. She felt no guilt about anything.

Entering the club, she bought a drink and walked up the stairs to the loft-like dance floor alone. She could feel the men's eyes following her. She wore black and silver to match with the club's chrome and black interior. The power of seduction filled her as she rotated her hips to the music while holding on to the stainless steel railing. After her performance, she usually ended up going home with some stranger, showing him a real good time. She put on a hell of a performance and ended up with more lovers than she'd ever imagined. It didn't hurt her finances either. Her mother had kept hounding her to get a job, but why should she bother when there was always someone to take care of her? She worked the contrast of her innocent appearance with her ravenous sexual appetite. The guys she met would give her money and an assortment of drugs in exchange for her talents. They were willing to do or give her whatever it

took to keep her happy. So far, she'd scored some weed, coke and Vitamin K, the street slang for ketamine.

One night, Doll was so involved in her performance that she failed to see Reuben enter the club. He sat hidden in the back and watched her turn on one of the patrons. When he saw they were getting too close, he ran onto the dance floor, angrily grabbed her arm and led her out back.

"So this is what you do when I'm not with you?"

"Come on baby, don't be mad. I was just warming up for you."

"Don't give me that bullshit! You trying to tell me you wouldn't have fucked him if I didn't stop you?"

"No, I would have come to you," she said as her hand enclosed his manhood. She felt it twitch. "Come on, don't be mad. We can do it right here if you want to. We don't have to wait. You'll like it, I promise." She emphasized her words by rubbing her body against him. Doll backed up and ran her finger around the outline of his throbbing tip, then pushed him against the wall and arched her back, pressing her lower body against him knowing that he could feel her heat. She tickled his ear with the tip of her tongue, then grabbed his hand and placed it between her legs. Reuben gave in and reached into the waistband of her jeans, just like she knew he would. They roughly switched places and he spun her around, hastily penetrating her from behind. They enjoyed a hot and hurried quickie and when it ended he sped to his basement apartment that Doll helped pay for with some of the money she "earned".

After a second vigorous session of no-holds-barred sex, they caught their breath and basked in the afterglow. Doll laid her head on his heart and gently twirled his chest hair.

She listened to his heartbeat as a plan began to form in her mind. She was sure she could have her cake and eat it too. But she needed to know more about him. All she really knew was why he'd been sent to Juvie and that he was endowed with eight thick inches.

"We never talk about the past. What was it like when you were a kid?" she started.

"Not much to talk about. Just me, my sister and Mom…Strugglin'."

"Where's your Dad?"

"Who the hell knows? Mom says the last time she saw him, I'd just turned two. Can we talk about something else, please?"

"You love me, don't you?"

"You know the answer. Why would you ask me this now?"

"Do you love me more than you hate Miguel?" she asked, referring to his mother's boyfriend, the one who hadn't died when Reuben wanted him to. She felt his body stiffen.

"I asked you to never talk about him."

"What if I told you I think I could do something that could release your aggressions, help you heal?"

Reuben rolled to his side and looked into her eyes. She didn't blink.

"There are a lot of people out there who would hurt others if they got the chance. That's why we need to strike first."

"Strike? What the hell are you talking about?"

"I'm talking about guys, women too, who are just as cruel as Miguel and Karl. What if we find them first, make them rethink their actions?"

"And how would we do that?"

"We could start by giving them a taste of their own medicine. We could kinda be like avengers, you know? Punish them for their bad deeds, their bad thoughts."

"But what if it's a good guy?"

"Nobody's that good. Besides, if it's not meant, it won't happen."

She stated that as if it were fact.

"I don't know, Doll."

"That's why you have me. This will be good for both of us. Trust me."

"What if we get caught?"

"I promise I'll work everything out to the last detail. It's what I'm good at." Intuitively, she pushed for more information.

"Hey, do you remember how good it felt when you jabbed Miguel with his own knife?" She could only imagine the feeling that knifing someone must give you. It had to be a stronger rush than shooting them. Something about getting so close appealed to her. She wanted to watch as the realization of death came over them. She wanted to be looking in their eyes when their souls leave. Doll added that goal to her itinerary.

♣♣♣

It *had* felt good when he jabbed Miguel with the kitchen knife. Reuben remembered the soft squish as it entered his

flesh. It gave him an adrenaline rush, especially when he heard Miguel yelp like the dog he was. No one, except the two of them, knew the real reason he'd tried to kill him. His mother's boyfriend sexually abused him every time they were alone. That's why stabbing him felt so good. For once, he was the giver and Miguel became the receiver. He wondered if the euphoria would be as strong the second time or if it was like a drug that you became immune to over time. Maybe, with her, he would learn the answer to that question.

"What's the baddest thing you ever wanted to do to one of your mom's boyfriends?"

All the therapy in the world didn't relieve the hurt or the anger that returned every time Reuben thought of Miguel.

"I wanna fuck him up. Make him hurt like he hurt me."

"How? What would you do? What have you dreamt of doing?"

"Making him my bitch, so he'd regret hurting us."

"Are you saying you want to fuck him?"

"Just to humiliate him the way he did me. I ain't no queer."

"If anyone knows that, it's me," she said and kissed him deeply, slipping her tongue between his lips.

"I can help you get what you want."

"How?"

"Well, if we can't find him, I'm sure there are others out there doing the same thing. You know that there are a lot of guys out there who would love to take advantage of a little woman like me. What if we turn the tables on them and I

bring them to you, then we fuck 'em up together?"

"I don't want them touching you."

"You know it would just be a way to get them for you."

"Why would you do that?"

"I'd do anything for you."

They bonded over his hate.

He'd never met a woman so small, dainty and yet so strong. Reuben couldn't believe that she'd chosen him. She was the antithesis of his mother and so different from all the other women he'd known during his short life. He felt a strong appreciation for her strength and would do whatever he had to in order to match it. He had to make sure she knew he'd always be there for her. They spent the next several days preparing for the main event. They talked endlessly about their plans.

"We have to be especially careful about fingerprints since we both have records. Even though they're sealed, we don't want to take the risk." She was a stickler for detail, so if a thought popped in her head at any given moment, she would jot it down and analyze it before she coordinated it to her satisfaction.

On Saturday, they divvied up the shopping. He went to Home Depot and bought 150 feet of utility rope while she went to Ace Hardware for large plastic lawn bags and masking tape. Together, they went to Kmart for an assortment of supplies, including several baseball bats, leather gloves and cheap rain slickers. He followed her down the aisle when she suddenly stopped and backed up, not stopping until she felt him sandwiched between her butt cheeks. He instantly wrapped his arms around her

waist and inhaled the scent of her Breck shampoo. Like an aphrodisiac, the aroma stimulated him and he leaned the lower portion of his body into hers.

"Save it," she whispered, stepping away and interrupting the moment. Doll continued to shop as if nothing had happened. He was aroused and thought of nothing else as he continued to follow her lead.

After leaving Kmart, the couple went to the Duane Reade drug store. She bought KY Jelly and he bought condoms. Anyone would have thought they were getting ready for a very sexy night. Their next stop was the Cigar Band, a small neighborhood storefront where Reuben picked up a couple of cheap cigars and a cigar cutter that resembled a mini-guillotine.

After purchasing everything on their list, they stopped at White Castle for a half dozen cheeseburgers, fried clams, onion rings and orange drinks. The shopping and anticipation gave them quite an appetite. They sat in the back so Doll could pour a half pint of vodka into their drinks to take the edge off. The thrill of anticipation spurred her on. While finishing their drinks, she leaned over and whispered in his ear.

"I can't wait any more. Let's go to Eddie's tonight and see if we can't hook us a fish."

The various scenarios played out in her mind a hundred times, like scenes from a B-list horror movie and she'd made sure she had everything they needed to deal with each and every scene. She was so ready and the thought of what would happen tonight excited her on every level.

She turned towards him and gave him a quick kiss. Closing the deal, Doll reached under the table and gently

ran her fingers along his crotch. She had the ability to make him feel like he was the only man on this planet gifted enough to satisfy her and as such, she knew he would follow her lead anytime and anywhere. He was her slave.

After dressing for the occasion, he drove her to the club. Upon entering, they immediately separated and casually walked through its industrial stainless steel décor. Looking more sinister than he realized, Reuben, in a black Henley shirt and black jeans, slyly glanced from right to left as he made his way through the boisterous crowd to the last table in the far left corner. He sat down, positioning himself between the dance floor and the club's lone security camera, turning his back to it so it couldn't record his face. He watched her go straight to work, seductively walking up to the bar and ordering a screwdriver. She looked sexy as hell in her silver miniskirt and black midriff blouse. She downed the first drink and ordered another, taking it to the small table next to the stairway that led to the dance floor. She held on to the slatted pewter railing, ascended the metal stairs alone and began a sexy undulation to the beat of the music. While she danced, she concentrated on Reuben as if he were the only man in the room.

Chapter Five

AFTER WRESTING WITH sleep for over an hour, Dominic got out of bed, showered and dressed. With attending school full-time, working a part-time job and studying whenever he could, he was too wound up and overtired to sleep. Besides, the college notified him that he'd completed enough credits to be an early January graduate which pleased his mother immensely. Maybe a congratulatory drink and some local distraction would help him relax.

It was the darkest of nights and that realization gave him a chill of apprehension as he walked the five long blocks to the club. He got to Eddie's a little before one. Things were still poppin' and Dominic relaxed as he walked in and settled down at the bar. He ordered a Heineken and once his eyes focused on the dance floor, she popped into his line of vision. The metallic silver of her short skirt caught his attention. She looked like the picture of innocence, yet with a sensual edge that showed in her choice of clothes and the way she slowly rocked to the rhythm of "I Am Your Melody", a smooth ballad sung by Spencer Harrison. Dominic found the combination irresistible.

She must have seen him watching her because, to his surprise, he watched her walk towards him. She squeezed

next to him into the tight space between him and the adjacent black leather stool. The slight pressure of her brushing against his knees felt intimate.

"Is this seat taken?" she asked as she slid up onto the stool without waiting for his answer or an invitation. Her deep, sexy voice was another thing he didn't expect from someone so young. It sent a chill up his spine and another part of his body began to react. She was smokin' hot.

Embarrassed, he tried to excuse himself. He didn't want her to see the effect she was having on him, but Doll grabbed his hand and pulled him close. Feeling his body next to hers, she came alive with the power that coursed through her body. It intoxicated her much more than the alcohol she'd consumed.

She led him to her table and offered to buy him a drink. He accepted, asked for a beer, excused himself and went to the men's room. She watched him leave. As soon as he was inside the restroom and the door swung shut, she opened and slipped the contents of two Vitamin K capsules into his Pabst Blue Ribbon. When he returned, he took a small sip, grabbed her hand and asked her to dance again.

"Finish your drink first." She coaxed and drank the remainder of her screwdriver to emphasize the point. "My turn, I'll be right back." He watched her head for the ladies' room and guzzled down most of his beer. When she came out, she had a few words with a guy who seemed to have been waiting for her. Dominic almost got up to help her, but only a few words were exchanged and she came back to the table. Doll grabbed his hand and insisted they get back on the dance floor when she heard Santana.

As he followed her, he asked, "What was that all about?" and nodded in the direction of the ladies' room.

"Some guys just think they can say anything to you. Don't worry, I promise you he won't make that mistake again. Well, at least not with me," she laughed as she raised her arm and made him twirl her around.

Doll didn't let go of his hand when the song ended. Instead, she led him out of the club's front door and took him around back to the alley behind Eddie's. He pinned her against the brick wall and was so intent on getting his hands up her skirt, he didn't notice Reuben slip up behind him. One solid hit with his leather and lead blackjack knocked the man out. The billy club once belonged to Miguel. Somehow, it seemed appropriate that he use it for this.

Doll went through the unconscious man's pockets, found his wallet and checked his license. *Dominic Brazza, a good-looking guy. Looks Asian and what?...Hispanic?...Black?* Her attention shifted as Reuben pulled the truck up to the alley entrance. She put the wallet in her purse. Together they dropped him into the truck bed where they'd made love a couple of weeks before. It was now lined with the plastic lawn bags they'd bought. Reuben attached them to the inside of the truck with duct tape so the bags were only visible when you looked directly over the tailgate into the truck bed. Besides, at one-thirty in the morning on a new moon night, it was pitch black, except for the dim streetlight at the end of the alley. That made his design ideal for what they had in mind.

Once Doll and Reuben got back to their basement apartment, they blindfolded and stripped Dominic naked. Together, they sat him backwards on a sturdy kitchen chair and tied his arms and legs around the back of it. His chin was propped up in the indentation made by the two black wrought iron scrolls that met in the center of the chair's

back. With a pillow stuffed between his stomach and the chair, they positioned him so that every orifice was theirs for the taking. Lastly, they ran the rope around his body and the chair several times to ensure that he wouldn't be able to move. When they were satisfied with their preparations, Doll surprised Reuben with a little coke she scored a couple of days before from one of her male friends. They did a couple of lines each and it was so close to pure that the high hit them both immediately.

"You did good, girl," Reuben declared. She kissed him, lightly sucking his tongue to show her appreciation of his praise. He gently, reluctantly, pushed her away and went to the sink for a cold glass of water. Instead of drinking it, he threw it into the man's face and got a sputtering reaction. It was time...

Hours later, after they finished abusing him, Reuben watched as Doll placed the plastic Pathmark bag on his head and tied the handles around his neck. Watching him struggle excited their bloodlust. As his breaths came slower and slower, they kicked the chair over and knocked him down to the trash bag covered floor. Reuben handed the knife to Doll and they each stabbed him once to see if he made a sound. Doll stabbed their victim in his right side which, with his Catholic background, strangely reminded Reuben of the soldier who stabbed Christ while on the cross. Pushing the thought aside, Reuben quickly got two bats and handed one to Doll. The two let out all of their fury on the poor man whose name only Doll knew. Both were disappointed by their victim's silence. When they were done, she grabbed the cigar cutter and a Ziploc bag, excited by the prospect of what she intended to do.

"Okay, how 'bout you get one hand and I take the other?" she asked.

Doll and Reuben clipped off the first section of each finger, using the crease line as a cutting guide and dropped the digits into the plastic bag. Then they wrapped masking tape around each finger, turning it into a contest to see who could do it the fastest. Doll easily won and when it was over she put the baggie in the freezer. Together they rolled the body up in several thirty-nine gallon lawn bags and carried him back to the pickup truck. They returned to Eddie's and dumped the body in the back alley where it had all started. On the way back to Reuben's studio, he turned to her.

"Next time I want to watch the life leave his eyes."

Doll slid closer to him and nuzzled his neck for two reasons. One, he *really* understood her and two, he'd said "next time".

The following morning, they woke up just before noon. Last night's escapade had been exhausting. At first, it seemed like a shared dream, that is, until they saw the remnants of the previous night. It had been wild, filled with wanton sex and murder, but the experience left them with a feeling of transformation. It had been a total turn on. Last night, they learned how well they worked together.

As Doll made scrambled eggs on the two-burner hotplate, she thought about all they'd done last night. *I think my favorite part, other than the killing, was when Reuben raped him from behind while I had him in my mouth.* She could still feel the power of Reuben's thrust, forcing the man deeper, almost to the point of choking her. She salivated at the exhilarating memory and felt the moist warmth between her legs. It was as if they became sexually connected in a way they never had been before. *Had it been*

as much of a turn on for him? She hoped so. That would guarantee it would happen again.

The thought aroused her to the point that she turned off the eggs and walked over to the bed where Reuben sat, putting on his Converses. She pushed him back, yanked down his sweatpants and sucked him dry before he knew what hit him. Satisfied, he lay there after she was finished and watched her go right back to the hotplate.

"Damn, I turned it off and the eggs still burned."

"Don't worry about it. I'll buy you breakfast."

Together, they cleaned up the tiny apartment and took everything down the hall to the incinerator in the unfinished section of the basement. Fire intrigued her since her pre-teens. She'd gotten away with burning things in her bedroom wastebasket. Once, she found an injured pigeon and set his wings on fire, reveling in the little bird's pain. Being burned also happened to be her greatest fear. Watching the flames as they destroyed the evidence brought back the nightmare…

Being estranged from Lark's family and so young, Doll couldn't remember whose funeral she had attended. It might have been her grandfather's or grandmother's. What she did remember was that was the first time she heard about cremation. Thinking about it, Doll thought going up in flames would be the way to go until the recurrent nightmares began. It started with her lying inside a coffin. People's faces swoop by for a very short time. She wonders why no one notices that she isn't dead and she tries to scream to get someone's attention, but everyone ignores her.

After the service, the casket cover shuts without warning and she feels the shaky movement of people carrying her. The thought of being buried alive terrifies her. At least cremation would be fast. She could hear the funeral home's staff as they remove the coffin's non-combustible materials like the handles, rails and latches and place the coffin on a conveyor belt. When it begins to move smoothly, she knows her destination. *Welcome to Hell* is her last thought as the metal rollers turn and she feels the rising heat. Her skin begins to melt…

Doll would wake up from the dream in a cold sweat with the corner of her blanket stuffed in her mouth. She didn't know how it got there, but she was grateful that it muffled her screams. She didn't want anyone to know her fear.

Holding hands like children in front of an autumn bonfire, Doll leaned her head on Reuben's shoulder until the stench of burning flesh and plastic became overwhelming. They thought about throwing the body into the incinerator as well, however, it was small and they were afraid the fire's temperature wouldn't be high enough to burn the body completely, thus leaving more evidence. Besides, that was too much like her dream. She's afraid of the flames, yet drawn to them like a moth. Doll reveled in fire's beauty. Fear and fascination are a powerful combination.

Not wanting their neighbors to smell the acrid odor, he shut the incinerator door and they walked back upstairs, arm in arm. Doll then handed him the victim's wallet. Removing the cash without even looking at the I.D., Reuben grabbed her hand.

"Come on, mi niña sucia, let's get out of here".

Chapter Six

SHEVAUGHN AND MATTIE left the doctor's office an hour later. On the way home they got Toni and Q from school, stopped to pick up a pizza and then drove to Shevaughn's. The four of them, including Kayla, now lived in a 1,300 square foot, three bedroom end-unit condo near downtown Portsborough, closer to the bookstore and the precinct, but almost an hour from Nonna's. They didn't see her as much as Shevaughn would have liked, but they spoke on the phone at least once a week. On her last visit, Nonna surprised her and brought a Mr. Elbers with her. He seemed to be a nice, slightly younger gentleman. The two met at one of the many church functions she attended. Suddenly, Lorraine had a social calendar and began having the time of her life. Shevaughn couldn't complain that their schedules tended to conflict. Nonna's new lease on life helped her get through losing Ariel and it was good to know she was enjoying herself.

A little envious, Shevaughn watched as everyone enjoyed their pizza. She couldn't join them unless she wanted a bad case of indigestion. She begrudgingly settled for some rather bland chicken soup and a fruit salad. After dinner, Toni and Q went outside to play with the dog. When Kayla got bored with them, she came in and they followed. Later, they all watched *The Cosby Show* and it

wasn't until then that she realized how tired she was. She looked forward to taking it easy.

By Friday, her fourth day of official maternity leave, she started going stir crazy. Shevaughn slept in and woke up to an empty house. She showered and marveled at her size as she gently washed her stomach. The baby kicked as if he was responding to her touch. *It won't be long now, little man.* She hummed as she put lotion on her body and selected her soft green chenille robe. She walked into their kitchen, tying the robe belt between her breasts and stomach. Shevaughn found the note Marcus left on the dove gray Formica countertop before he took Toni to school on his way to the bookstore. It read, "Take it easy, I'll bring you lunch". *He really does take good care of me*, she thought with a smile. However, instead of relaxing, she got busy and prepared a couple of advance meals for a later date. While the meatloaf and turkey breast pot pies were in the oven, Shevaughn puttered around the house, straightening up and lightly dusting. She went into the nursery to make sure everything was ready for her little prince. She had finished decorating it on day one of her leave.

When she was satisfied with her home's appearance, she got her baby magazine from the wooden rack and laid down on the couch. She placed her feet up on a stack of pillows and had just gotten situated when the phone rang. Shevaughn sighed and reached for it.

"Hello?"

"Von, it's Jared. How you feelin'?"

"Doin' good, how 'bout you?"

"I'm okay, I just got Dr. Spencer's report and I...I didn't want to ask you to come in, but I think you should see it."

"Why?"

"Let's just say this ain't no ordinary murder."

"You know I want the details. I can make it there...around two?"

"Good, we should have a few more lab results in by then. See you later."

When Marcus arrived with the chicken lo mein, Shevaughn was already dressed. As he walked in, he smiled and gave her an admiring glance.

"You look good. Going somewhere?"

"Jared called and asked me to stop by the office." She expected him to blow it all out of proportion and dug her heels in. His response surprised her.

"Ask him if he and Kennedy want to come over this weekend for a little dinner and cards?"

"Will do. Now let's eat before it gets cold," Shevaughn waddled into the kitchen. *That went a lot smoother than I expected!* Grateful, she got the plates from the cabinet and they sat down to lunch.

"You've been busy this morning," Marcus noted as he looked around. "What happened to taking it easy?"

"Two days of that was enough. Besides, I like taking care of our home."

"Long as you don't overdo it."

"I'd say don't worry, but we both know that's impossible. I'll be careful." They concentrated on their meal in silence. Shevaughn wondered if there was a little tension in the air or if it was just her imagination.

"You'll still be able to pick up Toni?"

"I should be. If I'm late, I'll call."

"Cool, well, I gotta get back." He stood up, put his napkin on the table, bent down and kissed her cheek. "See you around seven. I've got a late shipment coming in and I want to set it up before I leave."

"I'll have dinner waiting. Love you."

"Back atcha, babe."

Well, that went surprisingly well. Shevaughn cleared the table, put the dishes in the sink, added some dish detergent and ran hot water until they were covered. She promised herself she'd do them when she returned.

When Shevaughn arrived at the precinct, she exited the elevator and walked down the brightly-lit hall to her office. As she passed the tan file cabinets to her left, she heard a whisper so clear that she knew whoever spoke meant to be heard.

"I thought her old pregnant ass was on leave? Hell, she's been hoggin' the limelight for years. Folks act like she's the only homicide detective in the precinct."

Shevaughn's thoughts flashed red. *Son of a bitch! Who the hell is he calling old?* She realized the same ones who always hoped she'd fail were now the ones jealous of her success. She liked the feeling of triumph it gave her. *Girl, you have arrived.*

The sight of a young White man seated at her desk startled her. He jumped up and ran around the desk as Jared introduced him. Shevaughn gauged his height at about six four and he couldn't have weighed more than

one hundred eighty pounds. He resembled a gangly, overgrown puppy and looked uncomfortable with his size.

"This is my temporary partner, Officer Michael Walker. He's up for Detective in a couple of months and Captain Campbell thought it wouldn't hurt to give him a head start by showing him how things are done around here."

"Nice meeting you. Congratulations on your promotion."

"Your reputation precedes you, Detective Williams. I'm really honored to make your acquaintance. Your career has set an example we all need to follow." He held his hand out and Shevaughn shook it, flattered by his compliment. *That's exactly why the doubters are envious.*

"Geez, can you imagine how much butt he'd kiss if you weren't on leave?" Jared joked a little too loudly, even though he had to admit her wall of commendations and newspaper articles had tripled since the first day they met.

"Remember, it wasn't so long ago you were the rookie. You could learn some respect from the kid," Shevaughn teased. They both watched Walker blush and hurry back to his desk. His gait reminded her of Sesame Street's Big Bird. Shevaughn and Jared shared a look. *Were we ever that young?*

Changing the subject, Jared started talking about the case.

"We're still going through the missing persons reports filed this month, but it may be possible whoever it is lived somewhere else or hasn't been reported yet. I'll call Doc," he said as he picked up the receiver. "He wanted to be notified when you arrived."

As they waited for Dr. Spencer, Jared and Shevaughn

exchanged small talk. She invited him and Kennedy to dinner and cards and he accepted.

"I'll check with Kennedy, but I think Sunday evening would be best. I'm on duty Saturday night. We're still checking out a few clubs, looking for leads."

"This case got you going?"

"Yeah, so far we haven't even identified the victim. There haven't been any missing person reports that match what little description Dr. Spencer could give us."

"Well, you know even though I'm on leave, if you need me, just ask."

"You may regret that offer."

"Probably, but I mean it anyway."

Dr. Spencer entered the office, holding a thick file. As always, he looked like he stepped out of a magazine ad for spiffy seniors. He wore a gray pinstriped suit with a white shirt and silver tie.

"Afternoon, all. Von, you look like you're 'bout ready to pop."

"Then I look like I feel."

"You doin' okay?"

"I'm fine, just curious about what you found."

"Well, the victim is a twenty-five to thirty-five-year-old Hispanic male, about five feet, eleven inches, one hundred and ninety to two hundred pounds, but he was all muscle. It wouldn't have been easy for someone to take him down unless the attack took him by surprise. When my techs brought him in, I was surprised at the extent of the injuries. Almost every bone in his body was broken. He was beaten

so badly in the groin area that his scrotum was ruptured. The injuries look like they were administered by something cylindrical like a pipe or bat. Someone suffocated and beat him to death, almost simultaneously. The final blows were dealt post-mortem. Talk about overkill.

"I did the customary tox screen and discovered an unusual spike in the results, so I ran some additional drug tests. It showed positive for PCP. At first, I thought it might be Valium, but…Have you ever heard of ketamine?"

The three detectives nodded negatively.

"Ketamine is a drug more commonly used as an animal anesthesia. It binds to and blocks glutamate receptors all over the brain."

They looked at each other and the question marks were visible in their expressions. Dr. Spencer saw their response and explained further.

"It's a psychedelic drug that kind of disconnects the brain while paralyzing the body, similar to PCP or angel dust. He tested positive on samples from the inside of his mouth, stomach and blood, so he ingested it. Then, someone raped him every way possible. We didn't find any sperm, although it's apparent from the anal bruising that he was sodomized. We did find a miniscule amount of saliva on his penis which suggests oral sex. It's possible that the K-Hole, as it's referred to by users, actually enriched the stimulation. Some say it's like a near-death experience where it's like you're watching your body participate, but it doesn't feel like it's you."

"So someone slipped him a mean Mickey?" Jared asked.

"Doc, ya think this was a random pick? Someone was just at the wrong place at the wrong time? I mean, without

identifying the victim, we can't check into his history, we don't know if anyone had problems with the man or if he had problems with his job or home life."

"Well, it's just a guess. I mean, it's possible. The savagery suggests hate and anger. On a side note, I found an extreme variance in the force of blows. Some were so slight; it could have been due to hesitation, yet others were bone-shattering. So it could be one person who started off a little unsure of himself and picked up speed. Or he could have started out in a fury until he got tired. Then the blows became lighter. Oh, and later, someone had the presence of mind to remove the victim's fingertips, eliminating one source of identification. It looks like they used something like a cigar cutter since there's no evidence of sawing indicated. The cuts were perfectly circular; even a cleaver would have left variances in the cuts with different angles. No one could do it ten times exactly the same, yet these were. The victim's lividity proved someone moved the body after death, so we're either looking for a strong man or..."

"Could we be looking for a couple? I only say that because there were no signs of drag marks from the sneakers. I don't see someone doing it alone. He had to weigh what? Two, two fifty? Someone made preparations. Sounds like whoever's responsible for this did a little planning," Shevaughn surmised.

"Well, that would account for the differences in the force of the blows. We did find a few hairs and fibers. There were traces of seminal and vaginal fluid, so we know there was a woman involved. The lab should be able to confirm if the semen came from the victim when the results come in."

"And you say you found nothing on him or the dumpster?"Jared asked.

"There wasn't anything that we could identify as belonging to the killer or the victim for that matter, except the clothes we found him in. I did find a small Filipino sun and stars tattoo on his back, so I'm guessing that it may be his heritage or it could be something as simple as he thought the design was cool."

"So where do you go from here?" Michael asked.

"Well, we'll keep him on ice for a while, but unless we can identify the body within thirty days, I'm afraid he'll probably end up buried as a John Doe. Jared, I'm going back to the lab and if I come across anything, I'll let you know. Good seeing you, Von. Guess next time, I'll be seeing the two of you."

"Well, technically, you're seeing the two of us now," Von said as she touched her tummy.

"You know what I'm talkin' 'bout."

"Yeah, I know I'm looking forward to it more that you are. It'll be good to get back to my old self."

As Dr. Spencer started to leave the office, he bumped into Captain Campbell.

"Would you mind staying for a moment? I have something I'd like to share with all of you." There was no mistaking the look of satisfaction on his face.

After the customary greetings, he stood tall, cleared his throat and announced that the Democratic Party was considering him as a candidate for mayor. After a moment of shocked silence, Jared, Shevaughn and Dr. Spencer surrounded him, patting him on the back, shaking hands

and offering their congratulations. Officer Walker stood back and watched. A look of understanding passed between Jared and Shevaughn. This was why PR was always so vital to him. Suddenly, it all made sense. Campbell had his sight set on becoming a major politician and he'd done it well. The last five years under his reign were some of the best with only a couple of reports of any type of police impropriety. Internal Affairs were pretty annoyed with the lack of scandal.

Looking like a campaign poster, he was even patriotically dressed in a navy blue double-breasted suit with a crisp white shirt and a striped red and blue tie. Shevaughn wondered if she was next in line for Captain after he left. Although she wasn't the senior detective, she had closed more cases than anyone else on the force. At least, career-wise, things were finally looking up.

Chapter Seven

LARK GOT UP FROM the plaid loveseat and turned off the TV, a worried look creasing her brow. She hadn't heard from her daughter in days and now there was some maniac out there beating people to death. As much as she wanted to protect Doll, she had to admit that she was more than capable of taking care of herself. In fact, if she and the murderer ever came face to face, Lark's money would be on her daughter. Well, Doll had another meeting with her probation officer next Monday, so at least Lark would get to see her then. And this time she would insist that Doll and Reuben get a home phone. She felt the need to keep tabs on her as best she could.

She wondered what she could have done to change the way her daughter turned out. Sure, she was no June Cleaver, but she honestly believed she always had her daughter's best interests at heart. Lark always wanted to give her the world, however she'd gotten sidetracked when providing the necessities fell on her shoulders.

Doll was a latchkey kid until she entered high school and then, although she set her own schedule and got out of school by early afternoon, Lark hardly saw her. She thought it was due to all of her daughter's after-school activities and it was, except she didn't know that the activities were all related to alcohol, drugs and giving

head. She asked her neighbor to keep an eye on Doll and never got any complaints, but Lark wondered if Doll was doing something to keep the neighbor happy. Doll was her child, but Lark knew her daughter schemed to get whatever she wanted.

Doll never thought of herself as manipulative. It was just that she wanted what she wanted and didn't care what she had to do, or try to get someone else to do, to achieve her goal. It was all about feeling good. Even on those mornings that she woke up with a stranger, unsure of how she ended up where she did, she still had no regrets. Her biggest concern became what lie she would tell to keep folks off her tail.

Part of her probation was a bi-weekly visit with a therapist who spent time trying to convince her that her motivation stemmed from searching for a father figure. Doll thought that was psycho-bullshit. She didn't need a damn father figure, she didn't need *anyone* telling her what to do. *Everyone's working so hard trying to understand me. Hell, I don't even understand me.* She started missing her appointments and gradually stopped seeing the therapist. She would never admit to anyone that every night, before she went to sleep, she'd close her eyes and try to picture her father's face.

She often remembered the butterflies in her stomach the day a boy, close to her age, came up to her and started speaking to her. Sexual attention gave her the same feeling of excitement she'd gotten from stealing. As an early bloomer, she got all the attention she could handle. Although small-framed, she was almost a perfect size four, except she was slightly top-heavy. A C-cup at the age of

fourteen, her measurements were 34-26-36.

Doll found she enjoyed the challenge of the chase. As a freshman, she flirted with most of the boys in her high school until she met a senior who told her she was beautiful. The following week, he aroused her by sliding his hand up her mini-skirt. She decided he would be the one to take her virginity. They teased each other all week long and finally made plans to meet. On that Friday, after school, she met him under the bleachers near the baseball diamond. No one hung out there once the season ended. There, she performed her perfected fellatio technique. A powerful rush coursed through her body like an electric shock as she heard the boy moan. She was ready for him to take it to the next level. However, while on her knees, two of his friends joined the party. It turned out that he'd been bragging about their rendezvous. When he offered her to them, she refused. No one would treat her like that.

She fought like a wild cat and quickly learned she was no match for the three football players. Laughing, they stuffed a dirty gym sock in her mouth and held her down, letting her crush get first dibs. Then the other two took turns raping and sodomizing her. Near the end, they took the sock out of her mouth. Defeated, she remained quiet. They made her kneel facing one of them, bent her over and all three had her simultaneously; orally, vaginally and anally. They left her lying in the dirt after sexually torturing her for what seemed like hours. Doll never did remember how she got home. She didn't report the rape. Who would believe the high school whore? Plus she had initiated the original meeting. The three went unpunished.

Gossip spread throughout the school like wildfire and she was labeled the high school tramp. Her female classmates avoided her like the plague. *Might as well live the*

part, she convinced herself. Doll began carrying a purse complete with condoms and a cough medicine bottle full of whatever booze she could steal from her mom. She became a walking good time.

It wasn't until everyone started avoiding her and talking behind her back that she decided to give up boys and concentrate on older men. She carried on a three-month-long affair with her art teacher, Mr. Schneider, before the principal called her mom and requested she transfer to a GED prep school. Doll never felt guilty. The only thing that upset her was that the school informed her mother. That ended the affair before she had a chance to end it herself. She believed that everything should be on her terms.

Six months after the transfer, she'd had sex with at least half of the new school's male population. And she wanted more. That's when she went after Karl. It had been easy to get his attention and even easier to seduce him.

Doll spent the next several weeks in a state of anticipation. Although sex with Reuben was still good, it lacked the excitement of the night murder. She was finding it more difficult to climax without remembering that night, yet it didn't seem to bother him at all. Since all the newspapers had gone on to other newsworthy items in Portsborough and it looked as if Dominic's murder quickly became yesterday's news, she decided the time had come for another escapade. To soften him up, Doll made beef enchiladas and strong margaritas. After dinner, she joined Reuben and watched the fourth quarter of a Lakers game. Originally from Los Angeles, he would never give up on rooting for his team. Their win put him in a great mood. She put on her game face and leaned in close.

"You know what I've been thinking about? I'd like take a road trip to Philly and see my Aunt Morgan. Maybe on the way back we could pick up a hitchhiker or some poor sucker alone at a bar. You could have a girl this time if you want."

"You know you've never really talked about her. Is she your mom or dad's sister?"

"We're not related. She's my mom's good friend. Did I tell you she's gay? I spent a couple of weeks with her the summer I turned thirteen." Doll didn't mention that summer's experience. "We haven't kept in touch, but I'm sure Mom has."

"Well, I'm off Sunday, Monday and Tuesday. Do you want to leave then?"

"Sure, baby, that would be great. And don't worry, I'll take care of everything."

It took all she had to hide her excitement.

Chapter Eight

SHEVAUGHN FELT LIKE she was treading water. She didn't know how to make her husband understand, but she had to be more involved in this case.

"I just think Jared could use my help. Mostly I'll be fact checking, you know, paperwork. "

"Mostly? You said mostly. I will not have my pregnant wife chasing around town after some psychos."

"You're acting like I need your permission. I'm only talking about a few half days. I just can't sit here nesting while there's a maniac out there."

"You still think you're some kind of superhero? You know sometimes I want to check your closet for the cape. But there's no cape and you can't fly 'cause you don't have no damn super powers. You're my wife. What kind of husband would I be if I let you foolishly consider doing this...especially now? "

"Oh, I don't know...an understanding husband, maybe? You know this is me. I became a cop before I became your wife. I'm still me. Pregnancy doesn't change that, Marc. I'm not trying to be a superhero, believe me, but I do help people for a living. I find murderers and get them off the streets. Now, because I'm your pregnant wife, all of a

sudden you think I can just sit on my fat ass and act like none of this concerns me? I thought you knew me better than that. We better figure out a way to compromise because you're not going to win this one."

"So what are you saying? That you'd risk yourself, everything we have, to go after some maniac?"

"If that's what it takes."

"Well, I don't think I can sit here and wait while you're out there jeopardizing our future and our family. What about Toni? You'd throw away the chance to watch our daughter grow up? Did you even think about what losing you would do to her? She's seven, for God's sake."

"Now that's low. I'm doing this for Toni and all the kids like her. I know these victims were older but they were all somebody's child."

"Von, I swear if you do this, I'm gonna have to go. I can't sit back and watch. Not now."

"Go? What are you talking about? You're talking about leaving? I'm eight months pregnant and you'd just up and leave? Besides, where would you go?"

"I think Toni and I would be better at my parents' for a while."

"Boy, you ain't takin' my daughter no-damn-where."

Damn, two mistakes in one sentence. I called him 'boy' and said 'my' daughter. This is going downhill fast!

Then it hit rock bottom.

"Now, isn't *that* a nasty surprise? So if I don't agree with you I'm not a man? And suddenly Toni's your daughter -

not ours? Well, I don't think it would be very smart of you to take this to court. I wonder who'd they think would make the better parent? Let's see, a stable business owner or some delusional pseudo-Superwoman?"

Shit, now it sounds like I'm talking divorce. How'd we get this far this fast? Shevaughn noticed that Marcus wouldn't back down.

"We're going to my Mom and Dad's. You need some time to think."

"And you believe a separation is going to help us? What happened to the 'for better or worse' part, huh?"

"I didn't think that part would be based on a stupid decision."

"Stupid? Now I'm stupid?" The room got warm and Shevaughn knew they were getting close to crossing the point of no return.

"Okay, there you go. No, I didn't say you were stupid, I said your decision was and we're leaving until, or should I say, *if* you come to your senses. We won't be a part of this. I refuse to sit back and watch you make a bad move."

"Like leaving really solves anything."

"You know what I think? I think you're more concerned with getting another big case than your own safety. This could be another 'Ace' for you, couldn't it? Then you'd definitely be a shoo-in for Captain."

"What? Are you crazy? I never want to go through anything like that again, Captain's job or not."

"I'm not going to argue with you. I love you, Von, but if you go to work tomorrow, we won't be here when you get back. Now, good night, I'm going to bed."

"Whose?"

"What?"

"Whose bed do you think you're going to? If you're leaving, you might as well get used to sleeping alone."

"Fine, Von. I'll be in the den."

"Here, it gets chilly in there," she said as she rolled up the brightly-colored Kente cloth throw from the couch and tossed it at him. Marcus caught it, looked her dead in the eye and without saying another word, he turned and left the room.

Things had taken a detour and Marcus couldn't understand why. When they met, after getting over that first hurdle, she let her inhibitions go and fell for him. She'd been easier than he'd imagined. Some flowers and a little wine and dine was all it took and then she was his. Yes, he'd always have a problem with her job. He hoped that raising a family would make her look at things from another perspective, but she showed a side of her he'd thought about but hadn't seen. He worried that her job was more important to her than her family, more important than him. He hoped that the birth of their son would get her back on the right track, but for now, he would bide his time until she saw things his way.

He remembered the first time he saw her. It was just a glimpse, but he was struck by the fact that she was one of three Black women that he'd seen on more than one occasion on his Sony Trinitron 14-inch color TV The other two were Oprah and Jackie Joyner- Kersee. Both were out of his league...And then there was Shevaughn, definitely the best-looking of the three and local. She'd made a name for herself by becoming the first Black female homicide

detective. It started as a turn-on, a strong Black woman who was actually eliminating murderers from the general population. Everyone she'd come up against ended up dead or in prison.

It was God, fate or luck that put The Nook on her route home from the 23rd precinct. It couldn't have been any better if he had planned it. The first time she came in the bookstore, he was so nervous he pretended not to notice her at first, like that was even possible.

He closely followed her cases for years, clipping all the newspaper articles that mentioned her. When he made the "heartless" comment, he was well aware that it would probably get a strong reaction. He constructed that hurdle so they could get over it together and move forward with their lives. He did a little investigating and learned a lot from Eric and Jacques. Marcus kept everything hidden, especially now that they were a family. Shevaughn would come around and see things his way. She had to.

It was the first time they'd gone to bed angry and although she hated it, Shevaughn refused to give in. As she sat there fuming, her past forced her to remember all the lost ones; the kids she'd grown up with who'd ended up on drugs or dead because they didn't have family to look out for them. *There, but for the grace of God...*

She would fight for her marriage. Shevaughn never wanted Toni to experience losing a parent, although in reality she already had. And yet she knew she couldn't let the case go. The phone rang.

"Hello?"

"Hey, Von. Think you could come by tomorrow?" Jared

asked and then continued without waiting for her to answer. "Dr. Spencer says he'll have the skull reconstruction by then and there's this new forensic artist who's gonna try and give us an idea of what the victim looked like."

Shevaughn looked at the closed den door that separated her from the life she wanted to live. She knew she'd been blessed with another shot at love and a chance to have the family she'd lost as a child. As much as she would have liked to ignore the situation and let others handle it, she knew she wouldn't. She couldn't. *No sense in turning back now.*

"I'll be there by noon."

Running out of things to say, they ended their conversation, said good-bye and hung up. Shevaughn went to the master bedroom, got into their king-size bed and tossed and turned for a long fifteen minutes. Shevaughn couldn't sleep after the way she and Marcus ended their argument. She missed the warmth of his body against her back. She'd never admit it aloud to anyone, but she'd grown accustomed to falling asleep with his thumb encased in her fist. It had become her security blanket.

Sighing, she got back up, put on her teal velvet robe, stuffed her feet into the Daniel Green black satin slippers Marcus gave her last Christmas and went to peek in on Toni. She was surprised to see her daughter sitting up and reading in bed. Toni turned the book over, laid it down and patted the bed next to her, indicating Shevaughn should come and sit. She saw Toni was reading *Mother Crocodile* for the umpteenth time. The first book Marcus gave Toni remained her favorite and Shevaughn noticed that she usually pulled it out when something bothered her. Toni

reminded her of a little old lady and her daughter's head full of neatly arranged pink sponge rollers completed the picture.

"I thought you'd be asleep by now?"

"I couldn't, you and Dad were arguing." Although she said it very matter-of-factly, Shevaughn heard the catch in her voice and instantly felt guilty.

"It's okay, Sweet Pea, sometimes parents disagree."

"It's Sweet Tea, Mommy," Toni said referring to her name and the little joke they shared between them. She attempted a small smile, but they both knew her heart wasn't in it. "And I know parents argue or there would be no such thing as divorce."

Hearing the word said out loud caused Shevaughn to tremble as if from a sudden chill. She remembered that old saying, *'Someone walked over my grave'*.

"Believe me, it's not that serious." *Who am I kidding?*

"Really? You promise?"

"I promise. Now say your prayers and turn out the light."

"Can I pray that we all go to the arcade on Saturday? I need to work on my Frogger and Q*Bert scores."

The old lady vanished and her little girl reappeared.

"Save your prayers for more important things. I'll see what I can do." *Not if he's leaving in the morning. How am I gonna fix this?*

"Can I tell you a secret?" Toni whispered.

"Honey, you can tell me anything."

"Auntie Real says it's not your fault. You made a mistake."

"What?"

"She said you should have looked before you leaped. What does that mean? You went jumping somewhere?"

"When did she tell you this?"

"Last night…she stopped by and told me you need to be careful."

"I'm always careful, Sweet Tea."

"She didn't think so. She's worried for you."

"It's okay, Toni. It was a dream. I still miss her too." Shevaughn remembered Ariel gave her approval the first time she met Marcus.

"I don't know. It seemed pretty real to me. She didn't answer my question though."

"Were you frightened?" Shevaughn couldn't believe how unaffected Toni seemed.

"Of Auntie Real? Why? She'd never hurt me."

"No, she wouldn't." Shevaughn decided not to push it. "Well, if she stops by again tell her I'll be fine. Now it's time for you to go to sleep." She pulled the covers up to Toni's chin, kissed her forehead and then walked to the door. She turned just in time to see Toni roll to her side and look her in the eyes.

"Aren't you gonna ask me what my question was?"

"Okay, I'll bite. What was your question?"

"I asked if we were we gonna be okay."

The question stunned Shevaughn, but she didn't let it

show.

"She probably didn't answer because she knows we'll be just fine. You're too young to worry so much. Now get some rest. Tomorrow will be here before you know it."

Shevaughn flicked the wall switch down to turn off the light.

Filled with determination, she walked down the hall to the den and softly knocked on the door.

"Come in, Von." He patiently waited as she came to him.

She rushed to the black futon as Marcus sat up and wrapped her arms around him.

"Marc, can we at least try to work this out? We haven't slept apart since our wedding night and I can't go to sleep without resolving this. I love you and I understand your point of view, I really do. I'm just asking that you understand mine. I need your support. I have to help if I can and it has nothing to do with Ace or the possibility that I may be considered for Captain. This is what I do. I need to go to the precinct tomorrow. Would it help if I swear I won't leave the building?"

"You'll be behind a desk, no matter what?"

"Yes."

How long do you intend to stay?"

"A couple of hours...three tops."

"And you won't go to the crime scene...or the morgue...or the club?"

"I promise I won't leave the precinct."

"I don't know. I'm really not feelin' it ..."

"You need to trust me."

"I do, Von, with everything except your job."

"Marc, I'm asking you to take a leap of faith and back me up on this." She changed tactics. "Please come to bed. It's cold without you," she admitted and took his hand.

"So that's all I'm good for?"

"Well, now, I can think of a few other things..."

"Well, in that case," he grinned slyly, "we don't need to go anywhere."

Marcus kissed and touched her as he tried to make her feel the power his love had over her. He was rewarded when he felt her physically melt into his arms. Hiding the smile that played on his lips, he gently eased her down on the futon and buried his face into that part of her that convinced him years ago that they were meant to be.

Chapter Nine

IN HER DREAM, Shevaughn was walking along the shore of a beach. It felt so real she actually felt the white sand sifting between her toes. She looked down at the contrast of the sand against her dark chocolate toes painted with mauve polish. She then glanced up at the sapphire sky and saw a palm tree in the distance. She realized that her dream took her back to Maui. Two men stepped from behind the tree, one to the left and one to the right. They walked toward her, one dressed in white and the other in black. Happiness filled her heart as she recognized them both.

Wearing white, Tony approached her. With synchronized steps came Marcus in black. Walking at opposite angles as they approached her, they got closer to each other. She watched as their shoulders touched and they began to merge. For a moment their image seemed to alternate between the two of them until Tony disappeared and Marcus stood alone. He walked straight to her, enfolded her in his arms and kissed her. The kiss left her breathless. She felt the actual pressure on her lips and for a split second she was afraid to open her eyes. When she did, she gazed into the eyes of the one man who truly loved her…Tony. She suddenly broke the hold the dream had on her and hastily sat up. Shevaughn realized she didn't need

to analyze the dream before it faded. It felt as if Ariel was trying to tell her that something in her relationship with Marcus had gone wrong. The thought worried her. If it were true, then everything Toni told her about her conversation with Ariel made sense, but why did Ariel wait so long to warn her?

Shevaughn robotically went through her morning routine and everyone ended up where they were supposed to be when they were supposed to be there. Finally alone in the house, she sat at the kitchen table and finished her mint tea. Kayla walked in and as if sensing her mood, sat next to her. The dog got on her hind legs and lightly tapped Shevaughn on the knee with her paw to get her attention. She bowed her head and offered it for petting. She absent-mindedly scratched behind the dog's ears and somehow it brought comfort to them both. Despite that, Shevaughn felt a little off-balance as she headed to the precinct. The feeling seemed to increase when she walked in on Jared and his new partner. She sat at her old desk and frowned. She hadn't recognized that things would bother her so much until she watched Jared and... *Shoot, what's his name again? Michael,* leave to question Dominic's friends. She missed the chase and letting others do all the work just didn't feel right.

Her promise to Marcus held her back and Shevaughn wondered how long she would be able to keep it up and hold on to her marriage. Once again, doubt started creeping in. Look how some of her decisions had turned out; she'd shared a kiss with a stranger who ended her first chance at real love, she'd tried to help a victim and almost lost her daughter. She couldn't let her job jeopardize her marriage and the life she'd come to value so much. She knew what it was like to be alone and she damn sure didn't

want to go back to that. Besides, now she'd also have to contend with shared parenthood. With that, she thought about what Toni told her the night before. It wasn't strange that she dreamed about Ariel, but the message made her a little unsure and uncomfortable. Shevaughn sighed and went back to double-checking the missing persons' reports.

She had just started calling local tattoo parlors when her office door opened and a tall, stocky woman dressed in black stepped in. She looked as if she was already in mourning. Over six feet tall and a good two hundred pounds, Shevaughn was almost sure that once upon a time she had been striking and it probably hadn't been that long ago. Now there were lines on her face ahead of their time. She resembled the definition of haggard and as she slowly walked in, she brought the sorrow of death with her. Her eyes were red and swollen and Shevaughn could almost see the tracks of tears recently cried. With an uncommon certainty, they both knew the truth and her heart went out to the already grieving woman. She'd lost her child.

Shevaughn recalled the sick feeling she experienced when Toni disappeared and her stomach was in knots. She touched it and closed her eyes. *There, but for the grace of God…*She silently made a vow to herself and to this stranger. She would do anything humanly possible to help this woman find her son's murderer.

When the woman spoke her voice was surprisingly soft for someone so large. Shevaughn could tell she was having a hard time staying calm and her voice trembled when she began speaking before taking a seat.

"I can't find my son. He hasn't been to class or his part-time job in a week. I made a missing persons' report four days ago and no one has gotten back to me. I feel

something bad has happened to him. He would never just disappear without telling me anything. Please help me find him." She placed a small photo of a rather attractive man in tan khakis and a navy blue polo shirt on the desk and pushed it toward Shevaughn. There was no mistaking the family resemblance.

"I'm Detective Williams. Please sit down and let me try to help you," Shevaughn suggested as she got up and led the woman to the tiny loveseat along the wall.

"Thank you Detective. I'm Mrs. Brazza and that's my son, Dominic. You have to understand..." She spoke his name and the tears began again. "He's only been in trouble once for tagging and that was years ago while in high school. He's a good boy."

"You say you haven't heard from him in over a week?"

"Yes, we talked Sunday before last. I've been trying to call and the phone just rings. God help me, he's all I have. I'm so worried that he's somewhere hurt...or maybe worse, *huwag sana*." She lapsed into her native tongue.

"Can I ask you if your son has a tattoo in the middle of his back? A tattoo with the sun and stars?" She spoke of him in the present tense even though she believed he was the unidentified body in the morgue.

"Yes, he got it last year to honor his father and show pride in his heritage. The sun and the stars are symbols from the Filipino flag. You know where my Dominic is, don't you?"

Unfortunately, Shevaughn thought that she did. With Jared and Michael gone, she would handle this, even if it meant a trip to the morgue. She was already breaking her promise to Marcus, yet she didn't think twice about it. She

knew this would be the hardest day of Mrs. Brazza's life and she wanted to help her get through it.

"I'm going to make a call and see if I can help you. I'll be right back." She didn't want to do it in front of Mrs. Brazza.

Shevaughn contacted Dr. Spencer and warned him of the situation. He worried that the woman would not be able to recognize her son and he suggested that she see only the tattoo in order to spare her the gruesome sight. It was easier than explaining that the injuries were so severe that she wouldn't be able to recognize her own son.

In the scar or birthmark section of the homicide report, Dr. Spencer made a notation regarding a small mole on the left ankle of the victim's foot. Between that and the tattoo, maybe that would be all they needed to convince Mrs. Brazza that they'd found her son.

Shevaughn tried to explain the situation.

"Mrs. Brazza, I'm so sorry, but there is a possibility that we've located your son. For your sake, it would be best for you to remember him as he was. You don't want to see him like this, trust me. Do you think you could possibly identify him from the tattoo?"

"My God, you're telling me he's dead?" Mrs. Brazza sobbed as the answer to her question hung in the air. It felt almost tangible. She broke the silence and whispered, "I think I could. Dominic has a mole on his foot. If this person has both of them, it may be my son." Shevaughn, certain that the body had both identifying marks, knew the truth.

The ride to the morgue was somber since neither one of them spoke. When they arrived, Dr. Spencer escorted them to a private room set up for viewing. Dominic's body was laying on its right side with his back turned towards the

observation window. The attendant pulled back the white curtain. Dominic Brazza's head was covered with a sheet, yet the misshapen skull was still visible. Another sheet covered him from above his waist to his calf. The tattoo and the mole where the only things his mother could see, however, that was enough. Mrs. Brazza let out a shrill scream.

"Let me see my son!" she commanded.

"Please believe me, Mrs. Brazza. I'm a mother and you don't want to see him like this. You don't want to see what they did to him. Please, let me get you out of here."

"How can you say you understand while you stand here pregnant? There's hope in your life, but for me, there's nothing. He was our only son and now I have to go home and tell his sister that someone beat him to death."

"You have my sincerest sympathy, Mrs. Brazza. Is there anything I can do for you? Maybe have an officer escort you home?"

"No, I'll make it home. Can you see that my son...my son's body is sent to the funeral home? Can I call you with the address?"

"Yes, here's my card. I can make sure that's taken care of."

"Thank you, Detective Williams. You've been very kind. I apologize for my outburst. Here, I want you to have this picture of Dominic," she said and placed the snapshot in Shevaughn's hand. "I don't know how it can help..."

"There's no need to apologize. It's understandable under the circumstances." She took the photo. "It always helps to put a face with the name. Good bye, Mrs. Brazza. Please get

home safe."

Shevaughn fought the urge to give the woman a hug. Something told her Mrs. Brazza wouldn't appreciate the contact. Her pregnancy only served as a reminder of Mrs. Brazza's loss. Because of this, she backed away and watched as an officer walked Mrs. Brazza to the exit. She felt empathy for the woman and felt relief that the experience was over. She pushed the speed limit as she returned to the precinct. Suddenly, she had a bad feeling about leaving her desk.

As soon as she got back, she saw the message light on the answering machine. Instinctively, she knew Marcus had called after she'd left. While dialing him back, she prepared to tell him one small white lie. She hated to, however, it was necessary.

"Hi, hon, you called?"

"Yeah, were where you?" She could hear the suspicion in his voice. *He's checking up on me.*

"At the copy machine and then I had to go to the ladies' room. Your son is keeping me there today."

She knew mentioning the baby would improve his mood.

"So how's the case going?"

"We made some progress. We now know the victim's identity. That's why I was making a copy of his missing person's report. Is everything okay?"

"Everything's fine. Just wanted to know what you wanted for dinner."

"I've got this. I planned to take out the meatloaf when I get home."

"And you'll be home in an hour?"

"Yep, give me ninety minutes."

"Okay, I'll see you then. It's been really slow today, only sold two books and that was hours ago, so I'm gonna close The Nook early and come home."

"Good. How 'bout an early dinner and then maybe we can take Toni to the arcade for an hour or two? You know, I think our daughter is addicted to Q*Bert." She purposely said 'our daughter' to make up for her faux pas the night before.

"Cool! Maybe I could challenge you two to a game of Cyberball?"

"You know Ms. Pacman's my thing. I'm really not into football."

"Aw, come on. Just one game?"

"Well, we'll see. I'll be home soon. Love you."

"Back atcha."

She hung up, feeling guilty as hell, yet convinced that she lied for the preservation of her marriage. And that happened to be a very good reason.

About twenty minutes later, Jared and Michael returned.

"Well, guys, we now have the victim's name and address. Dominic Brazza lived only three blocks from the club, so I'm guessing he walked. His mother has been here and she identified the body. He was a Portsborough Community College student with no known enemies, no gang ties and no criminal record. Just a regular kid, so we have no idea why someone beat him so severely. There isn't an obvious motive. Oh, and his mother left this

picture. I made a few copies," she informed them as she passed the photos to Jared and Michael. "Let's spread his image around."

"I'll go back to Eddie's Lounge, show it around and see if anyone on the staff recognizes him," Michael volunteered.

"Yeah and I'll go to the college and see if I can find some of his friends and classmates. Maybe they can tell me something. Good lookin' kid," Jared observed as he clipped the photo to the inside cover of the case file.

"Yes, he was. Well, you two, I think I need to get ready to leave. I'll come back day after tomorrow unless something comes up between now and then." Shevaughn knew she needed to get home on time to avoid any foreseeable hassles from her husband.

Chapter Ten

DOLL AND REUBEN did the right thing and contacted everyone they felt should know about their weekend trip. Both cleared it with their parole officers, although neither of them mentioned their traveling companion since associating with a felon would be a parole violation. Several days before the trip, Reuben dropped Doll at her mom's house and went on his way to run some errands.

After he left, Doll asked Lark if she could get a few things to bring with her for the trip. After she was given her mother's permission, she excused herself and went upstairs. Reaching the landing, she took a detour and ducked into Lark's room. Doll went straight for the bottom night table drawer. Hoping that she would find the gun still there after all these years, she rummaged through it and found small metal box. To her surprise the box was filled with twenties. *Must be her rainy day money!* She counted it quickly and jammed the three hundred and eighty dollars into her pocket. Under the money, face down, was a photo. Doll turned it over and saw the image of her much younger mother sitting on the lap of a Black man with an enormously neat Afro. She stopped for a moment, turned it back over and read the inscription: *Lark and Joe, 1966.* A speedy calculation convinced her that the guy in the photo was her father.

She continued her search and came upon an old black stiletto knife with a spider engraved in red on the handle. When she touched the back of the blade it flew open and locked in place. She liked it. Doll retracted the blade, dropped it in her pocket and continued her search. *Where is it?* She looked under the bed and only found dust bunnies. She ran to her mother's closet and immediately saw the stationery box. She spotted it behind the VHS camcorder, which was sitting on the closet shelf in the corner next to the wall. Doll snatched the maple bedside step stool and stood on it, getting on her tippy toes, s-t-r-e-t-c-h-i-n-g until she almost fell. She grabbed a wire hanger from the closet rack and flicked at the box. It began to lean towards her and she quickly caught it before it made a sound. She rifled through the box and found the gun. Grabbing it and the box of bullets, she placed everything back where she found it and ran to her room. She rolled both items in a pair of jeans, added a sweater she'd left when she moved out, put the photo in her pocket and was back downstairs before Lark got suspicious.

"Mom, can I borrow the camcorder so I can video us with Aunt Morgan? We can watch it together when we get back."

Doll knew the camcorder belonged to Karl and that it probably hadn't been used since his death. When Lark replied, "Sure, why not? I think it's in my closet," Doll ran back upstairs to get it.

"You should probably make sure it still works," her mother advised when Doll came downstairs with the camcorder.

Satisfied she had everything she wanted from her mother, she took a moment and sat with her. They talked

for a couple of minutes and had a glass of grape Kool-Aid. When Lark asked how her job hunting was going, Doll's attitude changed to utter annoyance.

"I'm trying, Mom, but no luck so far. Get off my case, would ya?"

Faking anger, Doll got up and left to catch the bus or at least that's what she told Lark. Ten minutes later and two blocks from her mom's house, Reuben picked her up. They went home and began packing. Everything fell into place. *So far, so good.*

On the Saturday night before their road trip, their excitement made it difficult to sleep. When Reuben got into their bed and moved in to snuggle behind her, Doll turned around and surprised him with a deep kiss. They must have made love a hundred times, only this time it felt different. Usually their animal instincts took over and they went at each other roughly. Tonight, it was smooth and slow, relaxed. They melted into each other as if they were liquid and they floated toward one of the longest sessions of lovemaking that either one of them remembered. It was so good that for one moment they stopped and looked into each other's eyes. Astonished at the depth of her feelings, Doll knew that she'd been right when she decided he was hers. He did everything for her and she felt something close to gratitude as they climaxed together. Once they gradually separated and caught their breath, he began lightly kissing Doll from her shoulder down her left arm as the transistor radio on the dresser played Sade's "Sweetest Taboo".

"That was beautiful," Doll whispered, running her fingers through his hair as she listened to the words of the song. It felt as if a moment in her life was immortalized.

Something told her that tomorrow would be perfect.

They got up early Sunday morning and were anxious to get going. There wasn't a cloud in the pale blue sky. As they headed out, the day was sunny and cool. Reuben stopped at the Shell gas station and filled up the tank. As they got on the Verrazano Bridge, Doll turned up the radio and they sang until the station was out of range. Then she slipped the George Michael cassette, *Faith*, in the tape deck because she loved the song "I Want Your Sex". She played it repeatedly until they arrived in Pennsylvania. They saw a lone hitchhiker standing along the Jersey Turnpike during their drive. He looked cold and nasty. They looked at each other and read each other's minds, causing them to burst out laughing. He looked like a serial killer. There was no way they were going to pick him up.

They followed her mom's written directions until they pulled up in front of Doll's godmother's house. It looked exactly as Doll remembered. Aunt Morgan was sitting on the front stoop. Doll was surprised to see how much she had aged, but she tried not to let it show. She jumped out of the pickup truck and ran around the front to get Reuben, grabbing his hand. Doll made the introductions, proudly announcing him as her man. Aunt Morgan looked him over, gave Doll a sly wink of approval and ushered them both into her kitchen where she laid out a fantastic lunch. After washing up and eating lunch they spent some time together talking about the good old days. No one mentioned the episode that sent Doll home early. All they recalled were the happy memories.

Together they looked through old photos and reminisced.

"You were such a cute little girl," Reuben remarked.

"And I still am," Doll informed him, laughing.

"Well, I guess you two could probably use a nap after that long ride," Morgan offered.

"Especially after that great lunch, Auntie. Thanks."

"Sure, baby, anything for my girl. Doll, you can use my room. Reuben, I'll show you to the guest room. Do you understand there will be no cavorting in my house?"

"Yes, ma'am," Doll hastily answered.

Reuben grabbed her hand and pulled her within earshot.

"What's cavorting?" he whispered as he went up the stairs behind Aunt Morgan and Doll.

"Fuckin', silly," Doll answered.

"In that case, I can't wait to get home."

"But we just got here! You need to learn how to enjoy the moment."

Before going to their separate rooms, Doll gave him a quick kiss and gently brushed against his crotch after making sure Aunt Morgan wasn't paying attention to what she did. "It'll be worth the wait."

By the time Doll woke up the sun had already set. Anxious for their night on the town, she went into the guest room and kissed his soft lips until he was awake. He tried to pull her down to the bed with him, but she wiggled away.

"I think that qualifies as cavorting," she informed him. "Let's get ready to party." She dressed and waited for him

to come back downstairs. When he did, she saw he was wearing acid washed jeans and a waist-length denim jacket just like the ensemble she was wearing. The only thing that was different about their outfits were their shirts. He wore a MLB World Series t-shirt; hers was a multi-colored midriff top. After supper, they stayed to watch the Sunday Night Movie, but it was hard to concentrate when all they could think of were their plans for the night. As soon as the movie ended, they kissed Aunt Morgan goodbye and headed out to The Trocadero nightclub, located at 10th and Arch.

They waited in line to get in to the club. She stood with her back against him and his arms wrapped around her for warmth. She glanced at the building. Somewhere she'd read that it had a very impressive history dating back to 1870 and was listed on the U.S. Register of Historic Places *Just looks like some old building*, she thought, unimpressed.

A half-hour later, the line began to move and soon they were admitted into the club. Both went directly to the bar. She ordered a screwdriver and he asked for a rum and coke. Sipping their drinks, they found a table with a good view of the dance floor. She lit a long Satin cigarette and when she finished smoking, she asked him to dance.

"Shall we?"

He bowed and took her hand, leading her to the highly polished wooden platform that served as the club's dance floor as the beginning of "The Way You Make Me Feel" came on.

"I love Michael Jackson," she declared, grabbing his hand.

"I've got some of his moves," Reuben bragged.

"I bet you do."

Between dancing, talking, drinking and an occasional kiss, the evening passed in a flurry of various dance steps and featureless faces. Checking the crowd, they were surprised that there were more single men than women at the club. It limited their pickings, but it didn't stop them from having a great time.

The next thing she knew, Reuben was looking at his watch and commenting on how late it was getting.

"Ready to go?" he asked. Doll heard and understood the disappointment in his voice.

"Yeah, Baby, I'm sorry we didn't find someone for you tonight."

"Don't worry about it. Maybe we'll have better luck on the way home."

"You know what I'd like?"

"What?"

"Never mind. I'll show you on the ride back to Aunt Morgan's."

As they were leaving the club, a heavyset man bumped into her in the doorway. She began to express her anger until she looked up into the bulldog-like face of her old licking buddy, Wilbur. Instantly, she decided that Reuben would have to wait for his girl. This was meant to be.

"Well I'll be damned, if it ain't my old friend Wilbur. How've you been, man?" She wrapped her arm around Reuben and introduced the two strangers. Reuben still looked puzzled after the introduction.

"How did you say you know this guy?" he asked with a

confused tone of voice.

"I guess you could say Wilbur was my first boyfriend," Doll smiled seductively.

Reuben pulled Doll aside to prevent Wilbur from hearing their conversation.

"You want us to do him?" He did very little to hide his distaste.

"Yeah, I owe him that much. When I was a kid, he tried to take advantage of me and messed up my summer vacation." She didn't mention that she was a willing participant. "I got sent home early because of him. Now I want to take him as a souvenir."

"But you said this time we'd get a girl."

"Baby, would you indulge me this one time? Please? Next time we'll find you a PYT, okay?

"Make it two PYT's and you've got yourself a deal."

"You think you can handle three women?"

"I know *we* can."

"Okay, then it's a deal. Let's do this."

They went back to Wilbur. Doll made the suggestion that since she and Wilbur had a history that Reuben should let her take the lead. Reuben agreed.

"You know, you never did finish what you started that summer way back when. Care for a rematch?"

"What about your boyfriend?" Wilbur asked suspiciously. She got him in so much trouble that summer that he didn't want to go through anything like that ever

again.

"It's his idea," Doll lied. "Don't worry, he likes to watch. You game?"

She watched him lick his thick lips and waited for him to answer. When he didn't, she forged on.

"Do you live close?"

"Naw, I rode my bike."

"Cool, let's put your bike in the back of our truck. We'll give you a ride and get this party started. All we need is for you to give us directions."

Getting into the pickup, Doll situated herself between them for the fifteen-minute ride from the club to Hurley Street. She placed a hand in each of their laps, stroking them both to arousal during the ride. By the time they pulled up in front of Wilbur's house, they each had an erection. Wilbur's felt a little thicker and shorter than Reuben's and she was excited at the prospect of having them both.

"Nice house," she lied as she got out of the pickup. It was an older row house that needed a lot of TLC. The brick front was dirty and the exterior trim could have used a new coat of paint. There wasn't any greenery on the entire block.

"It was my mom's. She left it to me when she died of kidney failure last January."

"Where's your bedroom?"

Wilbur took her down the hall to the last door on the left. When he opened the door, they immediately saw what a slob he was. There were clothes everywhere and the clutter was mixed with old take-out containers and pizza

boxes. The room smelled like a herd of wild sneakers. Doll knew she couldn't stomach it for long.

"Where's your mom's room?"

"I haven't gone in there since she died."

"Oh, come on, man. This is a special occasion. Lead the way."

They walked back down the hallway and waited while he opened the door. She thought the room looked more like a hospital room than a bedroom. In the center of the room stood a double-sized hospital bed under a contraption attached to the ceiling. His mother once used it to pull herself up. The only personalization in the room was a burgundy chenille bedspread.

"You've been holding out on me. I've never done it in an adjustable bed. This is gonna be fun."

She started getting undressed in front of the two men.

"You got anything to drink?"

"I got some cold beers. You want one?"

"Yeah, you got three?"

"Sure, I'll be right back."

"Think you could find me something to tie my hands and feet with?"

Wilbur lumbered out, eager to please.

As soon as he was out of earshot, she confided in Reuben.

"I'll get his attention while you put the Special K in his beer, okay?"

She handed him the vial and Reuben placed it in the

front pocket of his jeans. He pulled out a two-foot piece of extension cord out of his back pocket and slipped it under the mattress.

Wilbur came back with three beers, strips of a shredded sheet and a large grin on his face.

"Can you go to the truck and get the camcorder from behind the passenger seat?"

"Why?"

"You'll see and I promise you'll like it."

When he left, Reuben spiked his beer.

Wilbur brought her the camera.

"Okay, put on some music, something slow and sexy. I'll give you two a little treat. You can even record it."

Wilbur turned his back on the couple and concentrated on the radio. He stopped when he heard the first bars of INXS's "Need You Tonight."

"That's okay?" he asked, eager to please.

"That'll work. Would you mind getting two chairs and bringing them in here? I want you both to have front row seats." Both men moved with the speed of lightning and the stage was set.

Doll moved to the music using her natural rhythm and sexuality to draw them in. She had their undivided attention as she slowly removed her clothes until she was down to her bra and bikini panties. Reuben filmed her performance. When Wilbur reached out to touch her, she deftly danced out of his reach and slapped his hand away. Near the end of the song, she took the camera from Reuben and handed it to Wilbur.

"You'll want to get this shot," she advised and sat on Reuben's lap. Doll softly sang the ending lyrics to the song as she moved in a circular motion while looking into Reuben's eyes. When the song ended, she made sure she spoke loud enough for Wilbur to hear.

"Damn, I've worked up quite a sweat! You know what? Let's take a shower together."

In the bathroom, she adjusted the water until it felt lukewarm. Doll knew men couldn't stand a really hot shower and she didn't want him in pain, at least not yet. She turned to Wilbur.

"First you get in, then me, then you, Reuben." She wanted to make sure his nasty ass hit the water first. "Turn your back to the water and I'll soap you up."

Wilbur believed this is what folks meant when they said they felt like they'd died and gone to heaven. He eagerly jumped into the shower and did whatever she asked. Doll wet the washcloth and soap and worked up a thick lather. She washed him like a big baby. She started with his face and then moved down his neck. She then scrubbed his shoulders and chest. By the time she got to his navel, the evidence of all her attention showed in his rock hard erection. Doll slowly encased it in her fist full of bubbles and began to gradually move her hand up and down.

He watched as Reuben's hands began to caress her body from behind. This was better than any sexual fantasy he'd ever imagined. Reuben slipped his fingers in between her legs from behind and she arched her lower body so that they would have full access. She turned around and faced Reuben, handing the washcloth to Wilbur. Horny and

impatient, he began washing her back.

"That's enough, Wilbur. Let's rinse off and we can really get this party started."

She and Reuben did the same and the three of them toweled each other off.

"Okay boys, let's go," she commanded when they were finished. She led the way back to Wilbur's mother's room. Once inside, Doll handed Wilbur his beer and got her travel-sized lotion out of her purse.

"So I'll smell good for you," she explained, putting lotion all over her body. Wilbur licked his lips as he watched.

"I bet your mouth is dry," she smiled and watched him take a long swig. She and Reuben walked to the bed and she put the lotion bottle on the dresser next to the TV. Using the sheet strips, he made slip knots and tied her hands to the bar hanging over the headboard. She lay spread-eagled, unashamed that the men could see everything she had to offer.

"Remember what you were doing when Aunt Morgan busted us?"

He'd had flashbacks almost every day. Wilbur rushed to the foot of the bed, knelt between her legs and burrowed his face into her sweet, clean treasure. He forgot all about Reuben and didn't see him quickly masturbate with the lotion. Wilbur thought Reuben might have been manning the camera until he felt Reuben grab his ankles and tie them to the opposite sides of the footboard. Reuben grabbed his left cheek and rubbed something cold between

Wilbur's buttocks. The next thing he knew, Reuben rushed inside him. It was a bit painful, but the rush of tasting Doll's juices had his head spinning. After the initial shock, Reuben's thrusts actually became intoxicating.

He started with slow, long strokes, but when Reuben's eyes connected with Doll's, he experienced extreme arousal and began using deeper and harder stokes. This pushed Wilber's tongue further into Doll and he sucked as if his life depended on it. Reuben held Wilbur down by his shoulders and made sure his mouth was deep inside of her as his thrusts grew harder.

"Gentle. Do it nice," she instructed, panting.

He felt extremely out of it and he didn't understand why. He'd only had one Sloe Gin Fizz, his mother's favorite drink, at the club and then one beer at home. He knew that he couldn't be drunk that quickly and from drinking so little, but he seemed to feel like he was floating and he couldn't get his thoughts straight. He kissed her breasts and went back down on her, leaving his posterior accessible for Reuben to continue to thrust deeply. In the heat of the moment it all felt so unreal, so intensified…and so good.

Doll pushed against Wilbur's chest while Reuben pulled him back. She sat up and bent over, putting her mouth around his dick, giving him head and fingering herself as Reuben continued his fearless thrusts.

As her orgasm started to build, she opened her eyes and nodded. Reuben slipped the electrical cord from under the mattress and wrapped it around Wilbur's neck. He lost all inhibition and began losing control, using the cord like a

horse's reins, riding Wilbur hard while cutting off his air. The gurgling sound he made as his eyes rolled back in his head turned Doll on even more and she peaked harder than ever. Reuben was so into the sex that Doll had to shout his name several times to get his attention.

"Stop! We want him alive for a while, remember?"

While he was unconscious, they freed her hands and put on their latex gloves. Together, they gagged him with one of the strips he'd brought them and tied his hands to the bar like hers had been. It took both of them to sit him up against the headboard. Doll used her mouth to put a new condom on Reuben. Then she knelt over Wilbur while Reuben entered her from behind. Wilbur slowly regained consciousness as she drew him in, so deep she felt him tap the back of her throat. This was just the way she liked it. Every time she felt him getting close to ejaculation, she would stop and prolonged the agony.

Reuben changed positions and Doll got up, went to her purse and took the gun and the switchblade. Handing Reuben the gun, she popped the blade out and stood close to Wilbur's groin. She touched his scrotum with the tip. He began to soften and she took him back into her mouth, sucking the life back into him. Reuben straddled Wilbur's shoulder and using his dick, lightly traced Wilbur's lips with his erection.

"Don't make a sound and you just may live," he lied. "If you want to taste her again, you'll have taste her on me. And no biting or she'll hurt you. Show him what you want to do, Doll."

Doll loved that he took the lead and she pushed the knife in until she saw a tiny drop of blood one of his testicles. She swooped down and licked it away. The effect

it had on Wilbur pleased her. She worried that the threat would make him soften, but the opposite seemed true. He looked ready to go again! She guessed that fear turned Wilbur on, but then again, he had no idea what they had in store for him.

Reuben rolled and pushed his hips in closer to Wilber's face. The feeling was more intense than he anticipated. At that very moment, he felt powerful enough to be a match for Doll. He pulled out before came and placed duct tape over Wilbur's mouth. Doll leaned over the bed and while looking into Wilbur's eyes, she let Reuben take her. The two climaxed hard. *Now for the fun part!*

They stood over him with her on Wilbur's left and Reuben on his right. Doll jabbed the stiletto into Wilbur's neck and handed it to Reuben who used the wound she inflicted as a starting point. He finished the job by cutting across Wilbur's Adam's apple, stopping just under his ear. The warm, arterial spray covered them and the air reeked with the coppery odor of blood. They were indifferent to the mess that was being created because, this time, they got the chance to watch the life drain out of Wilbur's eyes. Doll held her breath as she saw them go from fear, pain and panic to vacant. She didn't exhale until after she knew his pitiful soul no longer existed.

They left him there, tied up, lying on the hospital bed in his own blood. Doll had a flash of what she thought was sheer genius. She ran to the kitchen, found the largest butcher knife, came back and, with one swipe, castrated him. Removing the tape from his mouth, she stuck the appendage inside and then put the tape back in place.

"Since you like sucking so much," she laughingly joked. Reuben snickered with her. Just for the hell of it they took

their time and cut off his fingertips. They knew folks would instantly identify him since they planned to leave him there in his home. She couldn't resist using the cigar cutters again because she liked something about the faint snipping sound they made. She wouldn't be denied the chance to use them again. When they were done, they turned off the camcorder and returned to the bathroom to take a shower. Watching the bloody water spiral down the drain aroused them both and Reuben roughly pinned Doll against the frosted shower enclosure as they feverishly made love with the hot water streaming down his back.

On their way back to Aunt Morgan's, Doll made an observation. "You know what? I bet we end up a fuckin' legend or somethin'. You know, like the new Bonnie and Clyde, 'cept we don't rob banks and shoot folks, we rape and murder 'em. And nobody, man or woman, better mess with us if they know what's good for them because we're bad, baby. Bad to the bone."

Laughing, they high-fived each other.

"And you know that," Reuben affirmed.

They returned to Aunt Morgan's just before sunrise. Surprisingly, they felt energized and instead of going to bed, they quietly started preparing breakfast. Aunt Morgan, who had fallen asleep on her living room couch waiting for their return, woke up to the aroma of bacon and coffee.

"I didn't hear you two come in. Did you have fun last night?"

A sly glance of agreement passed between them and brought a smile to both their faces.

"Yes, Auntie. It was a blast."

Chapter Eleven

IT WAS ANOTHER Bid Whist night which usually meant good food and fun with family. However, as soon as Kennedy and Jared entered the room, one could feel that things were strained between them. After hanging up their matching leather jackets, Marcus was quick to enlist Jared's help getting the card table and chairs set up. Shevaughn took Kennedy down the hallway to show her the newly completed nursery. When they left the room, Marcus turned to his brother-in-law.

"What's going on, man?" Marcus asked.

Jared didn't even try to deny that they were having a problem.

"She's pushing the baby issue again. It's not like I don't want to have one, I just don't one right now. I mean, we just got married. I'd like to spend a little more alone time with my wife before the crumb snatchers start coming."

"Yeah, well, you know when a woman's mind is made up..."

"Yeah, but that doesn't mean I have to agree. We have plenty of time to have kids. I just want a little me time first. You know, everything will change once we start poppin' out babies."

"I see you need a biology refresher course. She's the one doin' all the poppin'."

"You know what I mean."

The conversation ended when Toni and Kayla entered the room. They were both wearing plum-colored hooded sweatshirts.

"Hey Dad, let's take Kayla out. Oh, hi, Uncle Dred. Where's Auntie Kennedy?"

Everyone knew that although Toni could say his name correctly, she preferred not to.

"She's looking at your baby brother's room with your mom. How my girls doin'?"

"Good, but I think Kayla needs to go potty. Wanna come?"

"Sure, you two, go on. I'll stay here. Give you a chance to catch up," Marcus suggested.

"Wanna see my Halloween costume when we get back? I'm gonna be Wish Bear."

"Huh?" Jared wasn't familiar with the character.

"It's a Care Bear, Uncle Dred. She's my fave. You don't know them?" Toni asked in disbelief. "Okay, I can 'splain it to you while we walk. I'll get her leash."

"Sounds good, teach." He turned to Marcus. "And while we're gone, maybe you can try to talk some sense into her," Jared whispered, nodding in the direction of their wives.

"Yeah, right. Now I'm a miracle worker."

"Hey, I could use all the help I can get."

"Okay, bro, but I've got one question for you."

"Bring it."

"Man to man, do you see yourself spending the rest of your life with my sister? You think Kennedy's the one?"

Jared didn't hesitate. "I know it."

"Then what's wrong with having a kid now? Of course, I could be a little biased, considering it's what Von and I have wanted for a while, but is the tension worth the wait? You know when a woman, especially my sister, sets her mind on something, it's already a done deal. I'd say just lay back and enjoy the process. I mean, you've heard the phrase 'happy wife, happy life'? I know it's corny, but it's also true."

"Okay, what's wrong with you two? The way things look, I'd say the honeymoon's over."

Shevaughn, like her husband, didn't beat around the bush.

"Why would you say that?" Kennedy dodged.

"Well, since you two arrived, you can cut the tension with a knife."

"I know I can talk to you, it's…well, we've been debating over whether or not to have a baby now."

"Debating or arguing?"

"Arguing, mostly. I don't understand why he doesn't want a baby."

"Is it he doesn't want one or he just doesn't want one right now?"

"Okay, he doesn't want one now. But I don't get it. This

is the perfect time. Look at us. I have my degrees, we both have good jobs and we're in a new home. What else does a baby need?"

"Maybe he just wants to spend more time alone with you. A baby changes things."

"Why does everyone keep telling me that? I know that. It's just...I think we'd be great parents and I want to start while I'm young. Von, I'm not doing this on impulse and I'm no stranger to acting on impulse. Like the time I asked Jared, 'Well, are you gonna marry me or not?' in the middle of our breakfast conversation. Boy, you should have seen the look on his face." Kennedy chuckled and realized she'd veered away from her topic. "I've thought it through. I don't want to wait."

"Well, my advice is do what you feel is right. You just have to get him to agree with you first." Shevaughn realized that's what she was trying to do in her own circumstances.

As the night went on, no one could ignore the elephant in the room. Conversation was tense. Trying to think of something to say while he dealt the cards, Jared accidentally blew Shevaughn's cover.

"Von, I never thanked you for handling the morgue identification the other day. I heard you handled it well, considering the circumstances."

"When did Von go the morgue?" Marcus stopped and gave his wife a puzzled look. She tried to avoid his glance. *What the hell? Well, it's too late now. The cat's definitely out of the bag.*

"Jared and Michael were out following a lead and a woman came in looking for her missing son. He turned out

to be the guy we found behind Eddie's Lounge. She insisted on seeing him and we needed her to identify the body, so I took her."

"So you left the precinct after promising me you wouldn't?"

"Marc, can we talk about this later?"

"Why? To give you time to think up another lie?"

"I said not now."

"Look, I don't want to be rude, but I think we need to call it a night. It's getting late anyway." Marcus stood and went to get Jared and Kennedy's coats.

"I'm sorry, Von. I didn't know," Jared whispered while Marcus was out of the room.

"No, you didn't, so there's no need to apologize." She tried to say it lightly, but it didn't match the sinking feeling in her stomach. There would be hell to pay.

As soon as Marcus ushered Jared and Kennedy out, he turned to face her. She saw he was furious.

"I knew I couldn't trust you whenever your job is concerned."

"That's not fair. It wasn't like I did something that put me in danger. What was I supposed to say? Your son's been missing for a week, but hold on until someone else can take you because my husband made me promise to stay in the precinct?"

"So that's where you were when I called? When you said you were at the copy machine?"

"I don't appreciate you checking up on me."

"Obviously, it's necessary."

"No, it's not. Come on, are we really gonna go through this shit again? That's exactly why I didn't tell you. I don't need this and the added stress can't be doing me or the baby any good."

As she turned away with the intention of leaving the room to end the argument, she felt a trickle of warm moisture run down her inner thigh.

"Marc, we need to go to the hospital. I think my water just broke," she calmly announced.

Marcus yelled for Toni, who came running into the living room with Kayla close behind.

Shevaughn let out a low moan as the first hard contraction hit.

"Mommy, you okay?"

"Sit down," he said softly, gently holding Shevaughn's hand and ushering her into the large black armchair.

"Toni, get Mommy a towel from the linen closet. I don't want to stain the chair," she explained to Marcus.

He stopped in midair and pulled her close. They felt the baby kick.

"I'm sorry, Von. This is driving me crazy. I've never acted like this before. I don't know why, but I seem to be 'what iffing' it a lot lately. I think it scares me."

"Baby, I'm scared, too, but it's a fact of life. My problem is I love you *and* my job. There's gotta be a way that both can coexist. I don't know what I'd do if I lost either." She held her head down and waited for the next contraction. "I think we need to start timing the contractions."

"Yeah, our son is the priority now." He smiled after saying the words aloud. "Stay here and try to relax. I'll get your suitcase. We'll be good to go in less than five minutes." She thought she heard a hint of regret in his voice. She wondered what he was thinking and wished he would tell her how and what he felt. *Why do men have such a hard time expressing themselves?*

The silence in the car was so thick that Jared couldn't breathe. He thought about the advice Marcus gave him. If only it were that easy...

It all started about a week after the day he'd gotten up the courage to kiss Shevaughn. She had slapped him and set him straight. On his way home, he'd stopped at an all-night diner for some of their made-from-scratch lemon meringue pie. He heard the screeching tires and got outside just in time to see a vehicle speed away. It cut across the diner's parking lot and struck a young woman. A blatant hit and run, the driver hadn't even tried to slow down. Jared squinted, trying to read the license plate, but it all happened so fast. Everything was a blur.

His attention immediately went back to the woman lying in the lot. He got to her just in time to see her move. Apparently, the car only clipped her. After looking her over, he was happy to report the injury was slight, but just to be on the safe side, he took her to the hospital. He carried her to his car, sped to the emergency room and waited until she was released. He intended to take her home, but she refused to go. She thought her boyfriend was the driver of the car that hit her. Jared checked her into a Howard Johnson's overnight and took her back to her apartment after she got a good night's sleep. When they

got back to her place, they noticed door was slightly open. Jared went in first to check the place and protect her. Her apartment looked like a war zone and what wasn't destroyed was missing. Her boyfriend probably skipped town.

Jared tracked him down on an attempted homicide charge and was present at his arrest. With his prior record, the boyfriend was sentenced to six years for a Class D felony. After the trial, Jared started to periodically pop in to check up on her after work. When all her bruises were gone, she turned out to be one sexy little number with a Latin flair. He'd slipped and fallen for the classic "damsel in distress" scenario hook, line and sinker. One night, she invited him inside her apartment to share some tequila and as the saying goes "one thing led to another".

When Jared woke the next morning, he didn't know what made him feel worse, the guilt of taking advantage of her or his hangover. He explained to her that this could never happen again, why it was wrong on so many levels and then they parted ways. He hardly gave her a thought until she called last month and said she needed to see him. It was very important. That was the day she introduced him to his son, a seven-month-old boy with his name. Shocked, he explained that even though he didn't want a relationship, he did want to be there to help support the child and made arrangements to send her a hundred dollars and fifty dollars a month. It wasn't much, but it was the best he could do, now that he had a new wife and home to maintain. And his new wife wanted a baby, immediately. Sooner or later, he would have to tell Kennedy about Jared Jr. How ironic it was that he'd been jealous of a dead man when Shevaughn named her daughter after Tony. Now he had a son named after him.

The old warning rang true. *Be careful what you wish for…*

Shevaughn, Toni and Marcus piled into the van and sped off towards Memorial Hospital. He'd made two practice runs last month and knew how to cut a good fifteen minutes off of the drive. They made all the lights and arrived in less than forty-five minutes. The nurses rushed Shevaughn into a room as she explained to them that she was in labor a month early.

Once he had Toni settled in the hospital playroom they had on the next floor, he went back to Shevaughn, holding her hand, giving her ice chips and encouragement. They breathed together and timed the contractions. When they'd first found out Shevaughn was pregnant, they'd agreed to opt for a natural birth. When her Ob/Gyn, Dr. Herron arrived, Shevaughn changed her mind and asked, or rather demanded an epidural.

After another four hours of labor, Darien Marcus Williams came into the world, looking dry and peeling like a tiny, shriveled up old man. Dr. Herron explained that the fluid slowly leaked out of the amniotic sac over the past month. However, if she massaged a little A & D ointment into his skin each day, he'd be just fine. Although a preemie, their son weighed in at a good six pounds, seven ounces. Marcus could hardly contain his excitement.

"I'm gonna call everybody and go get Toni."

While he was gone, Shevaughn breast-fed the newest member of the Williams family. As she looked into his tiny face, she re-affirmed her vow to protect her family and her marriage. Marcus found Toni and they hurried back to the hospital room. When they arrived, she introduced Toni to

her new brother.

"He looks like a tiny old Chinese guy," Toni noted, sounding a little unsure, as if maybe he wasn't exactly the baby brother she wished for.

"Lil' D's had a rough night. It's a hard job being born," Marcus explained. "He'll look better in a couple of days."

"Lil' D?" Shevaughn and Toni asked.

"Yeah, that's what I'm calling him. It fits."

During their ride home, Toni once again expressed her doubts about her brother to Marcus.

"How come he's not cute, like the babies on TV?" She sounded disappointed.

"Tell you what, let's wait a month and see how he turns out. He was born early, you know. He'll fill out and I promise he'll look more like the pictures you've seen."

"I sure hope so," she said with a dubious tone. Marcus squelched a laugh.

Chapter Twelve

NAOMI FULLER WALKED up to the door of her row house and immediately her stomach felt queasy. She wasn't sure whom she should call about the awful smell coming from her next-door neighbor's home. A couple of days ago, it reminded her of rotten garbage. Now it smelled like someone had the worst case of gas after a steady diet of beans, broccoli and eggs. She hastily slammed her front door shut, however the disgusting odor managed to sneak in and linger heavily in the air. As she inhaled, Naomi could actually taste the foulness between her tongue and the roof of her mouth. She involuntarily swallowed and ran for the bathroom. She didn't make it to the toilet and vomit churned out of her mouth as she arrived at the bathroom door. She couldn't take it anymore. This definitely qualified as an emergency. Without taking time to remove her coat, Naomi covered the lower half of her face with her sleeve. She tried to filter the stench as she went directly to her phone and dialed 911.

The Philly P.D. arrived less than a half hour later. She showed them to her neighbor's front door and waited as they knocked. When no one answered, she stood back and watched them use a battering ram to break it down. Several of officers immediately recognized the smell of death. It billowed outside like a cloud, forcing Mrs. Fuller to run

back inside her home.

Searching the house, the officers came across Wilbur's decomposing body as soon as they opened the door to the first bedroom. The temperature in the room was over eighty degrees. Someone forgot to turn down the heat. With the door and windows shut, the enclosed room accelerated the decomposition to putrefaction. His own mother wouldn't have been able to recognize him now.

The coroner arrived and began examining the body. Officers wearing latex gloves and photographers did their job, collecting evidence and taking photos. They all could see that fingertips weren't the only things Wilbur was missing. Two cops started to search the house, trying to locate the missing appendage, but came up empty.

"Can't wait for the wife to ask, 'How was your day?'" one of the cops joked to another.

"Yeah, I can hear it now, 'Oh, the usual, dear, spent some of it looking for a lost dick,'" the other detective replied. Both snickered and continued on their hunt.

Just as they decided that the killer might have taken it as a souvenir, the coroner removed the tape from the victim's mouth and even the most experienced boys in blue were shaken. A groan resonated through the air, riding along the foul stench. Wilbur's missing part was no longer a mystery.

The sound of her good friend's voice made Lark smile after she answered the phone, but her joy didn't last long. Morgan called to tell her about the police finding Wilbur's body in his mother's house. Lark immediately recognized

that his estimated time of death coincided with Doll's trip to Philly. In her heart, she knew it wasn't a coincidence. As soon as they hung up, she called Doll. Reuben answered and told her Doll was out at the store. After telling him a little about the murder, she instructed him to have Doll call her as soon as she got back. He quickly agreed.

"Sure, Mrs. McMillan, I'll make sure Doll gives you a call."

She thought she heard his voice tremble and she just knew that they had something to do with the murder.

♣♣♣

By the time Doll returned, Reuben was in a full blown panic. At the sound of her key in the door, he rushed to yank it open. He paced back and forth while he began his tirade, occasionally stopping to look into her eyes to gauge her expression.

"Your mother called and said they'd found Wilbur's body in his house and she was asking questions about our trip to Philly. She thinks she knows something. I knew it was a mistake to mess with someone you knew. What if the police put two and two together and connect it to us? The thought of going to jail, of losing you..." He suddenly stopped pacing in the middle of the floor and he looked as if he should have had a bright cartoon light bulb over his head. It was the first time he'd ever thought of the possibility of life without her. "There's no way they can connect this to us. We're just a couple of kids looking for a good time. To be on the safe side, I'll call my mom back and see if I can get anything out of her." Doll tried to reassure him.

Doll spoke with her mother for about ten minutes and hung up satisfied that Lark was none the wiser. Then she concentrated on calming Reuben down and taking his mind off the situation.

But this time, even though she was unaware, Doll was wrong about her plan. The phone conversation convinced Lark more than ever that Doll knew something about the murder. Her instincts told her that Doll's questions were more than idle curiosity.

When Morgan told her how someone raped, beat and murdered that poor boy, the first thing Lark thought was *God, help me*. Doll popped into her head. Lark went to the library and looked at several editions of the Philadelphia Daily News, but there was no mention of the murder. You would think something as vicious as what Morgan described would be on the front page, but honestly, no one paid attention to Wilbur during his short life. *Why should they start now?*

She sat on the sofa, took her mother's gold and crystal rosary out of her pastel multicolored seersucker housecoat pocket and prayed for strength. It had been specified in the will, that the rosary and a prayer were all Lark inherited while her two brothers and sister divided the eighty thousand dollar estate. She argued that she only wanted the money for her daughter's college education. Her siblings made a big deal of following her mother's wishes and she ended up with the rosary.

Afraid of how things would progress, Lark knew the situation would probably end with Doll behind bars again.

The burden of what she had to do next felt heavy on her body and in her soul. With a deep sigh, Lark shuffled to the phone and reluctantly called the police.

Jared lucked up on the Philly case. When he read the victim's fingertips had also been removed, he knew there had to be a connection to the Brazza murder. He had Michael contact the Philly police departments to see if there were any other comparable cases that might have gone unnoticed. Jared and Michael double-checked, but couldn't find any. For now, they only had two.

The media took advantage of the opportunity and were having a heyday speculating about the extreme nature of the crimes. They named the unknown suspects "The Fingertip Killers" and re-ran old stories of psychopaths and sociopaths with the familiar "beware of strangers" warning. Men wouldn't admit it, but they were suddenly extremely cautious about going anywhere alone. The crimes put a virtual stop to one-night stands. Men were now the hunted and although most wouldn't admit it, they didn't feel safe. Gun permit requests skyrocketed and the police were worried that the rise in gun possessions would contribute to someone accidentally getting shot instead of helping the crime rate. Portsborough was on high alert, expecting the worst. People couldn't help but remember and compare it to back in the day when Eric Becker had their town under siege. This time, women felt a little safer since it looked like whoever committed these murders only went after men.

♣♣♣

Shevaughn put the paper down on the kitchen table when she heard her son cry out. She couldn't believe all

this was going on without her. Sure, she loved being the mother of a newborn. There was something about that baby smell that really got to her, but working a murder case and catching the suspect, now *that* was her passion. She went into the nursery and picked DJ up. DJ stood for Darien Jr. Shevaughn preferred that to Lil' D. That nickname choice was all Marcus.

DJ was wet and hungry, so she changed his diaper, sat in the rocker and began to breastfeed. When Marcus came home on his lunch break and saw his Madonna and child, he was struck by what a beautiful portrait they made. He renewed his vow to keep his family intact, no matter what the cost.

Chapter Thirteen

NO MATTER HOW much Doll tried to reassure him, she couldn't help Reuben shake the feeling that everything was about to go horribly wrong. To appease him, she agreed to look for a new apartment. Doll thought he might be overreacting, except she believed in following instincts, so what was the harm in humoring him? Besides, she wanted to keep her man happy. It came in second to satisfying her every whim. Plus it gave her the opportunity to hunt in brand new territory. When she found the perfect spot they moved, but not before they gave the studio a thorough cleaning, just in case, to make sure they didn't miss leaving any possible evidence. Somewhere she'd read that hydrogen peroxide did a better job at removing blood, so they cleaned the apartment twice, once with peroxide and once with America's Choice bleach. The smell hung in the air as she went to the freezer to get her most prized possessions.

Their move turned out for the better because she found a small, one-bedroom garden apartment within the city limits of Portsborough. Reuben liked the apartment because they now lived closer to his mother, except it wasn't because they would visit. It was just in case they ever needed her.

In two days, he landed a job at the local pizza parlor

which supplied them with pizza for lunch and dinner a couple of times a week. They discovered that the only downside to their new home was the loss of the incinerator. *Oh well, you win some, you lose some.* She had more important things to think about, like planning for their next adventure...

♣♣♣

Shevaughn hung up the phone, excited. It was a good thing Jared called after Marcus left for the bookstore. He told her about a possible break in the case. She found it hard to believe that a mother thought her child capable of such crimes, yet she had to admit that it did seem suspicious that the victim and Dahlia Henderson knew each other from a past bad experience.

Unlike some, Shevaughn believed in the bad seed theory. Sometimes genetics dealt a lousy hand that may even skip a generation or two. If you didn't get it from your momma, you wondered about your great-uncle on your daddy's side. She knew there were some who, no matter what you did to stop them, ended up making bad decisions. They kept throwing the dice, even while on a downward spiral. Sometimes, they crapped all the way out. If they didn't learn from their mistakes, the road usually went downhill. Some learned, yet some didn't. Whoever beat those victims were racing down that road and they were mad at the world for ending up there. And if what Mrs. Henderson believed turned out to be true, her daughter truly qualified as a bad seed.

She immediately called Nonna to ask if she could come watch the baby while she went to the precinct. Happy to oblige, Nonna promised to be there within the hour, giving her time to call Marcus and get ready. She hoped he didn't

make it harder than it had to be and then she decided to avoid the tenuous situation altogether. Luckily, she got the bookstore's answering machine.

"Hey Hon, Nonna called and she's coming by to see the baby. I may take a moment to get out of the house and run some errands. Just thought I'd let you know in case I'm not home when you return." It was another white lie, but Shevaughn decided to save them both the tension. Besides, she intended to be back within the hour.

When she arrived at the precinct, Jared and Michael were waiting for her.

"Mrs. McMillan will be here shortly. We're trying to find Ms. Henderson, but she and her companion, a Ruben Mendoza, seem to have disappeared. We located their respective parole officers who confirmed they haven't reported in for the past two weeks. All we have their last known address, but their apartment is vacant and they haven't been seen around the neighborhood for a while."

"And you placed a stakeout at their last known residence?" Shevaughn wanted to make sure they had all their ducks in a row.

"They'll arrive as soon as the forensic team leaves. They're having a hard time coming up with any concrete evidence, said they noticed the distinct smell of bleach when they opened the apartment door. It looks like somebody cleaned up the crime scene pretty well. So whoever did this is familiar with police procedure when it comes to eliminating trace evidence. They're going over everything with a fine-tooth comb and believe me, if there's anything there, they'll find it.

"We've come to the conclusion that the first victim, Mr.

Brazza, saw himself as quite the ladies' man. It's possible that a woman lured him into a situation that resulted in his abduction. We've followed up by questioning all his known friends, male and female. But they all said that lately he'd been concentrating on his studies and his social life didn't keep him as busy as it usually did.

"Now, Mr. Wilbur Moss seems to be exactly the opposite. A quiet loner, the few people that knew him say he'd been diagnosed as slightly mentally handicapped. His mother took care of him until she died. After her death, his psychiatric social worker deemed him fit to live alone and take care of himself. A while back, a rumor circulated around the neighborhood that he'd tried to have sex with the young Ms. Henderson, although charges were never filed. Everyone we spoke to said they thought the accusation could be true. Moss seemed to be in a state of eternal puberty."

"So you're saying he tried to rape her? I've read her file. She was convicted of killing her stepfather for the same reason. No wonder she's angry. I need to talk with her parole officer and her therapist."

"She went to her therapist the first month she was released, but other than that there's no record of her seeing a psychiatrist after her release from Juvie."

"You're kidding me. That wasn't a condition of her parole?" Shevaughn shook her head. "Did they think all her problems would vanish when they set her free? The system failed big time by letting her slip through the cracks. Someone should have been keeping an eye on her."

She remembered the havoc Terri caused after her release from Blackstone. Not only had she been going to therapy, but Shevaughn also personally kept an eye on her.

Sometimes, watching isn't enough.

Interrupting her thoughts, Captain Campbell breezed in. Today he looked like the casual version of a campaign poster, wearing navy Dockers and a blue and white polo shirt. Following close behind were Mrs. Campbell and a young man wearing an expensively tailored black Armani suit. Both Captain and Mrs. Campbell's features were present in the young man's face.

Mrs. Campbell was attractive and mature woman who Shevaughn thought bore a striking resemblance to the aviator Bessie Coleman. She wore a red dress with white piping to complete the patriotic color scheme.

"Look who passed the bar in the top ten percentile," Campbell announced proudly as he entered the office. He was carrying a bottle of sparkling apple cider. "The wife and I wanted to introduce you to our son, Sharrod Campbell, Esquire." He sounded like a wrestling match announcer. "You know what my son said to me? 'Dad, I want my first case to be pro bono' and he pledged to do at least one a year! Most kids coming out of college are only thinking about how much money they can make, but not our son. Our son wants to donate his services to some poor defendant who wouldn't ever be able to afford him. That's my boy." Honest pride filled his voice.

Lately, Campbell was more interested in politics than policing and complaints had been spreading around the precinct like wildfire. Everyone could see that his priorities were more about his future occupation than his current one. His son, the attorney, completed the perfect political family picture. Everyone in the precinct shook hands with or patted Sharrod on the back and shared the cider. They toasted the new attorney with coffee mugs and paper cups.

On his way out, the captain pulled Jared aside.

"Can you explain to me why I got a call from Internal Affairs regarding you sleeping with someone you met on a case?"

Jared immediately knew who the Captain was referring to.

"Sir, I can explain. It didn't start out as my case, I just happened to be there when the hit and run occurred. It's a long story."

"Well I don't have time to discuss it right now, I'm taking the family out to celebrate, but I can't wait to hear your explanation. Let's get together in the morning so you can update me on that and the Henderson case." The captain knew some folks in the department were complaining about him neglecting his present duties and he wanted to squelch any vicious rumors before they got to the press.

Less than an hour later, there was a light tap on Shevaughn's office door and Lark McMillan shuffled in. Looking like she hadn't slept in weeks, her beige London Fog trench coat had seen better days and so had she. Her pale gray eyes were red-rimmed and swollen. Her complexion was so pale it lacked any sign of color, as if someone drained all her blood. Shevaughn's instantly felt sympathy for the woman.

"Mrs. McMillan, please come in. Have a seat. Can I get you anything; coffee, soda, water?"

"No, thank you. Wait, a little water would be nice. I..." She looked puzzled as if she'd forgotten what she wanted

to say.

"You came in to tell us about your daughter, Dahlia Henderson, right?"

"Legally she's Dahlia McMillan, but after everything that happened between her and her stepfather, Doll decided to take her biological father's name."

"What exactly happened between your husband and your daughter?"

"He attacked her and she shot him."

"You were a witness?"

"No. I was asleep in my bedroom and ran to her room after I heard the first shot. I heard the second shot before I could get up the stairs. She and I fought over the gun and once I got it from her, I dialed 911," Lark lied. *Now's not the time to change your story.*

"Have you noticed any changes in her behavior? Has she been moody, angry?"

"I thought she was on alcohol or some kind of drugs every time I saw her after she left Juvie, but I don't see much of her since she moved out to live with her so-called boyfriend. His name is Reuben...Mendoza, I think. What's bad is, as much as I hate living alone, I'm more comfortable now that she's gone."

"Do you think he supplies her with drugs?"

"I have no idea where she gets them from."

"Okay, let's get to why you're here. You feel she has something to do with Wilbur Moss' murder?"

"I think it's strange that he was found dead after their weekend in Philly. It's a little too much of a coincidence."

"Did you see them after they returned? Notice anything out of the ordinary?"

"No, not really. I guess you could call it women's intuition. What I'm saying is that it's possible."

"Okay, so what led you to that conclusion?"

"I have nothing concrete, but my daughter has a mean temper and she thinks she's smarter than everybody else. I think she believes she can get away with murder."

Shevaughn was surprised at the lack of emotion Lark showed while accusing her daughter of such a heinous crime. She was sure Lark wasn't aware of all the gory details. *How do you handle thinking your daughter is a monster?*

After getting the information and a recent photo from Mrs. McMillan, Shevaughn sent her home with the promise that if they found anything connecting her daughter to the murder, they would contact her. She got in touch with the court that presided over the Mendoza case to see if either of them had expunged or sealed their juvenile records. They hadn't and Shevaughn asked them to fax a picture of Mendoza to her.

Jared notified the Philadelphia police and they immediately went to Morgan Crawford's house and questioned her about the likelihood of her goddaughter's involvement. Although she told them she found it hard to believe, she did admit that if Lark thought it could be a possibility, she would be inclined to agree with her. Convinced that they needed to talk to the couple, the department put out an APB on both and enlisted the media's help in locating them.

♣♣♣

The following day, all the major newspapers and TV stations in New York and Philadelphia ran pictures of Doll and Reuben. The reports stated that they were wanted for questioning. Doll was livid.

"Where the hell are they getting their information?"

"My guess? It's your mom. What we gonna do now?"

"I think we need to lay low for a while. Our faces are plastered everywhere. You go in Friday and pick up your check like everything's cool and we'll make our getaway."

"What if somebody recognizes me? I'm not going to jail for a measly hundred and fifty dollars."

"Well, I still have some of the money I got from Mom's. It'll have to hold us until we think of something."

After hiding for a week, Doll and Reuben were getting edgy and paranoid. They decided to get out of town and take a trip to Atlantic City for a little pick-me-up and eager to lose themselves on the crowded boardwalk. Hoping they might run across their next conquest and get the chance to bring them home, Doll prepared the apartment for their return and gave Reuben the small plastic bag of pills.

On their way to Jersey, Doll and Reuben hit the jackpot when they stopped at a 7-Eleven station for gas and beer. They came across a tall, thin, milk chocolate-complexioned brother sporting a goatee and several tattoos. He was accompanied by a woman that looked to be about five four and one hundred forty pounds.

"You promised me two girls this time."

"I know, baby, but we can't look a gift horse in the

mouth. These two are ripe for picking."

She'd never been with a Black man and wondered if the myth was true. "Have you ever had a Black girl? I mean look at her, she's sexy, right?" Reuben nodded in agreement and pulled up in front of the couple. Doll hopped out of the pickup to greet them.

"Fix them a beer."

Reuben dropped a Quaalude into the beer can and handed it to her.

"Hey, where you two headed? My name's Dahlia, but folks call me Doll. That's my guy, Reuben, behind the wheel."

"We *were* on our way to Atlantic City, but my car broke down and the mechanic says it's gonna take five hundred dollars to fix it. We only have half, so we figured what the hell? Let's hitchhike and see if we can win enough to get it fixed. Anything else we win would be gravy."

"Get out! That's where we're headed! How cool is that? Can we give you a ride? We could use the positive vibe."

"And it's cool with your boyfriend?"

"Yeah, he'd like the company. So, what's your name?"

"Grady Evans and this here's my lady, LaShawn."

Doll bought them to the passenger window and introduced them to Reuben. They all couldn't fit in the cab of the pickup, so she graciously offered to ride in the bed of the truck with the couple.

"Hey, do you guys...?" Doll brought her thumb and index finger together, touched her lips and inhaled, giving them the universal sign for smoking a joint.

"Umh, yeah, we've got some on us."

"Keep it. I've got some Thai stick. Just make sure you hold it down. We don't want someone seeing us and reporting it to the cops."

Doll handed them a joint and the beer.

"I promise it'll make the three-hour ride shorter. In fact, I was thinking, before we get on the road, how 'bout a little get-to-know-you going away party? You know, have a couple of drinks, couple of joints. She nodded in Reuben's direction.

"He'll have to be the designated driver, so no drinks for him. I do make a hell of a margarita. We should go back to our place for a while."

The two nodded "yes" as they passed the joint between them. When they gave it to Doll, she eagerly accepted and inhaled long and hard to make them feel more comfortable with her. She waited and watched for signs of the drug taking effect. It didn't take long.

Under the influence, the couple's eyes were glossy and bloodshot. They appeared dazed. As soon as she was convinced they were feeling no pain, Doll knocked on the back window of the pick-up and signaled Reuben to go back to their apartment. He made a fast U-turn and headed home. It was almost too easy. *Like a walk in the park.*

It started out pleasant enough and having the additional woman made it all the more interesting. After a few drinks, LaShawn became a willing partner. The guys were treated to a show with the two girls fondling and kissing each other. Doll came up to Grady and got close, slowly grinding her body against him. When LaShawn saw what was happening, she went to Reuben and did the same. All

four were hot and bothered in no time.

Grady walked to their queen-sized bed, pulling Doll with him. Tying his feet to the spindle footboard, she placed kisses up his leg, stopping only to admire what he was working with. She crawled further up and secured his hands to the headboard while she brought herself in contact with his mouth. As he tasted Doll, LaShawn crawled between his legs and placed Grady in her mouth. Reuben came up behind her, grabbed her around the waist and entered her, placing himself as far in as humanly possible. They became an endless gyrating mound of lust. At one point, Doll and Reuben looked each other in the eye. He knew what she wanted and they rearranged themselves so she could have it.

At first, it bothered him that she was so set on having another man inside her, but he kept it to himself and planned his next move. She would show her appreciation later, when they were alone. He watched as she rode him and had to admit the scene was making him hot. Reuben grew harder as LaShawn sucked him and he heard Doll moan. She rocked atop the man, enjoying every inch this stranger had to offer. They lost themselves in the pounding strokes.

Doll's orgasm came swiftly. When they switched positions, Reuben carefully added extra KY jelly to his throbbing member. He watched Grady kneel over LaShawn while she gave him a blowjob and Grady buried his face between Doll's legs. This gave Reuben access to what he'd been waiting for. He wanted to punish Grady for satisfying Doll and began by slowly easing his way in. There was a momentary resistance and a muffled protest,

but it was swept away in a tsunami of lust and Reuben's persistence. Soon, all four were totally immersed in the debauchery. Reuben let go and came first and Grady swiftly followed suit. The girls brought each other to a final climax. Exhausted, they fell asleep with the hitchhikers in the middle of the bed, Doll in front of Grady and Reuben behind LaShawn.

Close to one that next morning, Doll gently shook Reuben's shoulder and woke him. She handed him the stiletto and showed him that she had the gun.

"It's time to finish this," she whispered.

Simultaneously, they woke the couple up from their slumber.

When Grady first opened his eyes and looked down the barrel of the gun, for a split second, he thought she had to be joking. Hell, he'd done everything they wanted him to. There was no need for threats. He reached up to brush it out of his face, but she returned the gun back into position and he realized she wasn't trying to be funny.

Next to him, LaShawn awoke to the prick of the knife on her throat.

"Get up you two," Doll commanded. They did as they were told. LaShawn started to reach for her clothes on the floor.

"Don't bother, you won't need them. Let's all go to the kitchen. Try anything and I promise you, you won't make it. "

Grady grabbed LaShawn's hand.

"Aw, ain't that sweet? It's a little late to be protecting

your lady," Doll informed him. "Move it." She poked him with the gun as she grabbed a pillow from the bed.

When she turned on the light in the kitchen, they saw that someone had been busy while they were sleeping. The linoleum floor was covered by two large tarps.

"Lay down." The couple began to protest, but she cut them off.

"You know I'll use this, just lay down. There's a tarp for each of you."

LaShawn began to cry softly and buried her face in Grady's shoulder.

"We did everything you wanted, why would you want to do this?" He asked, putting his arms around her.

"Because we can," Doll answered flippantly. "Now I suggest if you have anything else to say, it should be in the form of a prayer."

Grady lunged towards Doll and Reuben swiftly stepped in to protect her. Even though he understood the man's instincts, he could not let him hurt her. Reuben jabbed the stiletto into Grady's stomach twice, in, out, in, out. It all happened so fast. The three of them watched him fall to his knees. LaShawn screamed and knelt in front of her boyfriend, frantically trying to stop the heavy flow of blood from his wounds.

"You can't do this! You can't just kill us," she protested, screaming.

On the tarp, facing each other, Grady clutched LaShawn and pulled her close.

"I love you, baby. Now I want you to close your eyes and keep them closed," he instructed as he ran his

fingertips over her eyelids. LaShawn did.

"Aw, protecting her 'til the end...How romantic. Now kiss each other good-bye."

As their lips touched, she closed in with the pillow. It muffled the sound of the two fatal gunshots to their heads.

Doll and Reuben were up the rest of the night. They did their fingertip ritual, adding the new ones to the collection in the baggie. Together, they rolled each body up in a tarp and went over the apartment, making sure there wasn't any evidence of what transpired within the last twenty-four hours. She went through the clothes on the bedroom floor and found a total of four hundred and fifty dollars in the pocket of his jeans. That was more than Grady said. *Lyin' bastard*, Doll thought as she put the money in her purse. Then, exhausted, they went back to bed and slept soundly until the alarm went off at four-thirty in the morning.

Doll and Reuben got up and placed the tarps in the truck bed. They left the two corpses in separate locations; Grady beneath an underpass on I-495 West near the Jersey border and LaShawn in the marshes near JFK Airport.

During the ride back to their apartment, Doll matter-of-factly announced, "Know what? I think we need to go see Mom later today."

Reuben could not ignore the warning bell ringing inside his head. He knew she wanted to kill her own mother! For one short moment, he thought about the possible consequences and knew their souls were destined for Hell. Once again he wondered if what he did made any sense. Was she worth it? But he couldn't help himself, he loved

her and the answer was yes...she was. At least they'd spend eternity together. Besides, he knew when Doll put her mind to something that there was no talking her out of it. She had to have her way. While driving, he took a side-glance at her delicate profile. He would do whatever she asked. As if reading his mind, she put her hand on his arm, lifted up a little to her left and gave him a kiss on the cheek.

"You know I love you, don't you? You can ask me anything. I'll do whatever you want." She emphasized her statement by placing her hand in his lap and softly caressing him. He couldn't argue with her. That's exactly how he felt.

Chapter Fourteen

AS SHE SAT down to her lunch of split pea soup and a BLT sandwich, the doorbell rang. Lark looked through the front door peephole and saw Doll and Reuben standing there. Her heart began to pound loudly. She hid her apprehension, not wanting to show Doll her fear and let them in.

"Hello, Mom." Doll greeted, sliding in past her. Reuben remained in the doorway. A look passed between Lark and Reuben and a small shiver swept over her body. He looked upset, almost sick. She turned to face her daughter.

"So have you been, Mom? Had any interesting conversations with the police lately?"

"What are you talking about?"

"You sound confused, kinda like the night you shot Karl. You remember that night, don't you? The night I saved your ass and we lied for you? And this is how you repay me...by going to the police, telling them about us? That's not the way to show gratitude, *Mom*. Is it, Reuben?"

Doll and Lark looked at Reuben as he slowly shook his head "no". *It's as if Doll's pulling his strings!* Something about that realization made Lark more uncomfortable.

"What happened to your manners, *Mom*? Invite my man

in." Lark remembered the last time she heard that sarcastic, commanding tone in her daughter's voice. It was the night she murdered Karl.

Reuben turned, shut and locked the door behind him. Somehow, the everyday sound of the soft click of the lock bode ominous to Lark. He walked past her, their faces mere inches apart. For a split second, they stared into each other's eyes and the look in his eyes scared her even more. *He's afraid, too!* Then the moment passed and he stood at Doll's side. Only then did Lark notice the gun in her daughter's hand. She recognized Karl's Ruger. *It's supposed to be in the box in the closet. When and how in the hell did she get it? Why didn't I check when I heard about Wilbur? But then again, he hadn't been shot, so why would I?* Panicked, she looked at the kitchen entrance, wondering if she could reach it and get out of the back door before Doll squeezed off a shot. She didn't think so.

"You'd never make it, believe me." *Now she's reading my mind?* "I think the basement is better for what we have in mind. Let's go."

The pair separated and came towards her. Doll stood on her left and Reuben on her right. They each took an arm and escorted her to the basement door. Lark struggled out of their hold, let out a scream and tried to make a run for the back door. They went after her. Reuben grabbed both her arms and Doll hit her in the face with the gun. Lark reeled from the pain and when she could see past her tears, Reuben stood over her, holding a familiar switchblade.

"Quiet! Don't make me use this," he whispered. As they took her to the basement door, Doll's tone went from threatening to polite.

"After you, Mom. You know what they say...age before

beauty." Doll followed closely behind her mother, poking her in the small of her back with the gun. Reuben followed. Doll hit the light switch at the top of the stairs and the three descended into the finished wood-paneled basement.

"Take a load off," Doll instructed, pulling up an old office chair for her mother. Lark sat, all the while trying to think of a way out of this mess she'd gotten into.

"So, exactly what did you tell the cops?"

"The cops? I didn't tell them anything."

"Don't play with me, Mother." Lark heard the warning in her tone. "Reuben, give me the tape."

Lark watched as he removed his backpack and dug into it, coming up with the silver duct tape.

"Doll, listen to me. There's no need for you to do this. Doll...Please, I don't know what you're thinking. I'm your mother. Why?"

"Because you're a traitor. I saved you from prison and now you think you can send me there?" Doll asked as she took the knife from Reuben and cut off two pieces of tape. She roughly wrapped it around Lark's wrists and the arms of the chair. "What did you tell them?"

"Not much, I swear. I just confirmed what happened that summer in Philly."

"So you gave them a motive?"

"They already knew all about it. I couldn't deny what happened. Doll, for God's sake, don't do this. I had to tell them the truth or they would have known I was lying."

"Yeah, we all gotta do what we gotta to do. So I guess that's why I've gotta do this." Doll cut off a smaller piece of

tape and placed it over Lark's mouth. She turned to Reuben.

"Honey, go to the garage and see if Mom has any gasoline. She usually keeps a can in there for the lawnmower."

♣♣♣

"Gasoline? Why?" He didn't like where this was headed. *She wants to set her mother on fire?* He dealt with raping and killing strangers for her, but to kill your own mother, the woman responsible for giving you life?

"Come on, baby, don't give me a hard time. Well...not 'til we're done." Doll chuckled at her implication.

"Are you serious, Doll? We've done a lot together, I mean, you know I'm here for you, but..."

"Whatever I want, remember?" He watched her walk towards him. She stopped when she got less than an inch away from him and looked up into his face. "We take care of each other in every way. It's a trade-off, you give me what I want and I do the same for you. That's what love is." She leaned in, put her hands on both sides of his face and pulled his lips to hers. Reuben felt the heat of desire emanate from her body to his and once again, he forgot about everything but her. "Go through the back door in the kitchen." When she released him, he turned and once more, his feelings for her overruled his conscience.

As soon as she heard the door shut, her attention went back to Lark.

"You see, stupid bitch? He'll do anything I say, anything I want him to. He loves me. Is that why you called the police? 'Cause I've got a man and you haven't had one

since you killed that sorry bastard of a husband way back when? Or is it 'cause you couldn't satisfy Karl like I could? You had to try and ruin everything for me? Now, I have to make sure they don't get nothin' else out of you. You can't blame anyone but yourself for what happens next. I'd say I'm sorry it's come to this, Mom, but I think that somehow we knew it would end this way. You see...you've made me what I am today. "

Lark listened to her daughter rant and tried to think of something, anything to stop Doll from doing what she intended. *How could this have gone so wrong?* Maybe Doll was right. Maybe the day she let her daughter take the blame for Karl's murder was the beginning of their end, but somehow she thought it started way before that. However, if she'd been strong then and accepted her guilt, she probably wouldn't be in this mess now. She should have told the truth and accepted the consequences. She'd set a poor example and now she was going to pay.

Reuben returned with a five gallon red plastic gas can and handed it to Doll. She shook the can and Lark heard the liquid slosh against the bottom. Lark thought hard about how much gas was left in it and realized that it had to be less than half full since it wasn't grass-cutting season. She never filled the can up until the first signs of spring. It wasn't safe to have a full can in the garage for months. She prayed that it was almost empty.

"Hon, I don't think this is enough. See if you can siphon some out of the truck." Lark hadn't considered that option. As she watched Reuben walk back up the stairs, her prayers changed. She asked God's forgiveness for all her sins and accepted the inevitable.

Doll ran upstairs and grabbed Lark's purse, checking the wallet. She found almost fifty dollars and some change. Angry there wasn't more, she ran back downstairs with the large tan leather tote in hand.

"Is this all the money you have?" She screamed as she wrapped the purse handle around her hand and beat Lark in the face. When she removed the tape, Lark closed her eyes and refused to speak. Incensed, Doll went to the laundry room in the back of the basement, picked up a laundry basket full of dirty clothes, returned to her mother and dumped the clothes at her feet. Doll began spreading them by kicking them around the chair.

"Did you know I've always had a fear of fire, Mom? And I still played with matches every time I was alone and I was alone a lot, wasn't I? After school, sometimes whole weekends, while you were out having a good time or probably hunting for a man. Did you even care what happened to me while you were out there whoring around? Remember when you'd wait for me to go to sleep and you would sneak out? You gave a key to the next door neighbor, Mrs. Connors. After all these years, the memory is still fresh. Did you know her husband would take the key and sneak over to the apartment after you left? At first, he just touched me, but soon he wanted oral sex. Don't worry, he never fucked me. I always wondered why not. We did everything else." Doll knelt in front of her mother, using the dirty clothes to cushion her knees as if reliving that moment so long ago. "Do you know when I sucked my first dick? I was eight, *Mom*, EIGHT! Now whose fault is that? Why weren't you there to look out for me?"

When Reuben returned with the full can of gas, she got up, took it and circled around her mother. She doused the pile of clothes with gasoline while humming "Fire" by the

Ohio Players. Lark hoped her eyes would silently convey for her to stop, but if they did, Doll chose to ignore it. She reached for the lighter in her pocket.

"You can't do this, Doll," Reuben warned. "You can't do this to your mother."

"Honey, go wait in the car. I'll be right out."

"Please, come with me, baby. She's learned her lesson. She won't talk to the police anymore, will you Mrs. McMillan?"

"I know she won't. Now please go sit in the car, Reuben," Doll answered for her mother.

He reluctantly went back upstairs and she turned her attention back to Lark, retaping her mouth.

"If you thought he was gonna save your ass, you're dead wrong." Doll flicked her Bic and stared into the tiny flame.

"Yeah, I *used* to be afraid of fire, except not today 'cause this time it's doing what I want it to. They won't be getting any more information out of you," she said, nonchalantly lighting the pile of dirty clothes at her mother's feet. The flames rose quickly. Lark began to feel the heat and then came the excruciating pain. Her cries were muffled behind the tape, yet they sounded so loud in her head that she almost didn't hear her daughter's goodbye.

"Well Mom, gotta run. Can't keep my man waiting. I'd stay if I had some marshmallows." Doll's laughter seemed to hang in the air after she left. It was the last thing Lark heard as it mixed with her inner screams and the crackling fire.

Chapter Fifteen

ON HER WAY home from her six-week checkup with Dr. Herron, Shevaughn dropped by the precinct with DJ in tow. She'd gotten a clean bill of health and she was ready to focus on something other than her new son. A content child, he only cried when wet or hungry. Most of the time, he cooed and gurgled to himself, fascinated by his feet. He recognized his family and got especially excited whenever Toni came into his view. She now thought of him as the best thing since peanut butter and jelly. When he looked up and smiled at his sister, you could see her heart melt.

He looked especially adorable in his jeans and his baby blue long-sleeved shirt and sneaker booties. A tiny Mets baseball cap completed the outfit. When they first came home from the hospital, she tried dressing him in baby clothes and the sight caused her to laugh until she hurt. He resembled a miniature senior citizen in a Halloween costume.

With DJ in his carrier, sitting front and center on her desk, most of her brothers and sisters in blue that were on day shift stopped by to check him out. After all the oohs, ahhs and "old man" comments, they left the two of them alone in her office.

"Well, Mr. Popular, let's see if you're still dry," she said,

sticking a finger in his waistband between his diaper and baby-soft skin. He wasn't, so she changed him and gave him a bottle. While feeding him, she stared at the whiteboard with the scribbled timeline of the last hours of Mr. Brazza and Mr. Moss. Witnesses placed Brazza at the Portsborough Library, studying until after six. He left after several of his buddies suggested they go out for a beer and he bowed out, claiming to be tired. They just assumed he'd gone home. The next day, he lay dead in an alley.

What happened between then and morning? She assumed he went home like he'd told his friends. *And then what? Maybe he got a second wind, went out for a drink and ended up at Eddie's?*

He wasn't a small man. No one picked him up and carried him away, so he was probably lured out of the club. Dr. Spencer thinks the murder weapon was a baseball bat. Can't imagine anyone walking around with a bat unless it was totally hidden, but how could he use it without Mr. Brazza seeing it first? Then odds are he didn't. The first blow was probably from behind while something or someone distracted him.

They'd shown Dahlia's photo to the bar employees and patrons. A majority said they thought they saw a small woman who resembled the picture. She'd made quite an impression on several of the men when she danced. No one remembered Reuben, let alone a bat. One guy in particular said she'd been very rude to him and described what she had on. Regretfully, he didn't see her leave. The security cameras were practically non-existent and the ones that everyone could see were highly visible. The owner had them installed mainly for show. Even after the lab worked on them, the images were so grainy that Shevaughn doubted she would have been able to recognize herself in the photos if she had been on camera.

They'd gone through all the collected evidence and found that their sources were all cheap and local. All of the blood samples matched with the victims. A few hairs had been found, except none of them had the roots attached, so the best they could do was try to match them to the victims. All of the hair samples matched the victims except one.

There wasn't any additional information on Mr. Moss. No one could recall seeing him days before his body was found. It didn't look like he had any friends. He did have a social worker that stopped by every other month to check in on him and make sure he was still competent to live alone, but she had seen him days before his calculated time of death. They found he worked a part-time job at the local supermarket to supplement his disability check. His final paycheck still waited for him.

These two victims couldn't have less in common, yet something had drawn the killers to them. Convinced that there were two people committing these murders, she always thought in the plural, one male and one female. There had to be something everyone missed. *What the hell is it?* Shevaughn had the bad feeling that if they didn't figure it out soon, more bodies would add to the count.

Jared rushed into the office looking like the precinct was on fire. He woke DJ who had been sleeping peacefully until the door slammed. Shevaughn picked him up, placed him on her shoulder and gently patted him on the back.

"Sorry, Von. Jersey police just found the body of a male stabbed in the stomach with a gunshot wound to the head and someone reported seeing a red and white pick-up truck leaving the vicinity."

"What's that have to do with us?"

"It looks like he was raped before he died and the coroner found vaginal fluid on his person. Just like the other two male victims. The only difference is he'd been shot."

"And not beaten? So, you're saying there's a connection? I'll call Mrs. McMillan and see if her daughter has access to a gun."

"She did when she shot her stepfather," Jared reminded her.

"Yeah, but that was years ago. We can't jump to conclusions," she warned.

"Von, Reuben drives a red and white pickup and the victim's fingertips were missing."

"Why the hell didn't you say that to begin with? Got me cussing in front of my baby." She put DJ back into the carrier and dialed Mrs. McMillan's number. It surprised her when a man answered the phone. She remembered the woman mentioning she didn't like living alone.

"This is Detective Shevaughn Williams, Homicide. I'd like to speak with Lark McMillan."

"This is Deputy Fire Chief, James Nolan. I'm afraid she can't come to the phone. It appears Mrs. McMillan was the victim of a house fire...she'd dead."

"It wasn't an accident, was it?"

"Not likely. Someone restrained her with duct tape."

"Okay, we have a lead on this and we'll update the information on the APB," Shevaughn said with a slight nod in Jared's direction. She hung up as he amended the order to add the fourth victim's name. No more than ten minutes after completing the amendment, they got a call from the

Port Authority Police Department who reported finding a young woman, shot dead, with missing fingertips. That brought the total to five; three male, two female.

Bodies were coming in a lot faster than anyone anticipated and now they were coordinating investigations in Philadelphia and Queens105[th] precinct. Although the attention of all the law enforcement agencies focused on the same couple, it looked like the two had vanished off the planet without leaving a trace.

Chapter Sixteen

DOLL COULDN'T BELIEVE they were highly publicized fugitives already. Their pictures were everywhere. Reuben shaved off all of his facial hair before they cautiously left their new apartment. It took years off his appearance, making him look even younger. They moved what little they had in the middle of the night. On the way to a motel on the outskirts of town, they stopped at a drugstore to buy hair dye, scissors and some personal supplies. Wearing a scarf and sunglasses, she got out of the store without recognition. However, she worried that someone would be suspicious of a girl wearing sunglasses at night.

When she got to the cashier, she noticed the girl behind the register was a tiny little thing, just like her, except maybe a little taller, a little heavier and with jet-black hair. Doll took the resemblance as a sign. *Everything happens for a reason.* She went back to the hair supplies aisle and exchanged it for a darker shade. After Doll made her exchange, Reuben drove them to the motel.

She waited in the pickup and let Reuben check in. He returned with the key to an end room with a view of the back of the parking lot. The dingy room contained a small kitchenette in the corner with a mini-fridge on the counter. She opened the door and put the baggie in the tiny freezer

section at the top.

"Don't you think we need to get rid of that?" Reuben asked with a disapproving look.

"Why?"

"Just think it's crazy carrying evidence around with us. You know the police will be looking for them. What did you do with the tape?"

Doll realized he was probably right and although she didn't want to destroy the Wilbur tape, it would be the smart thing to do.

"Okay, I can let them go and we won't do it anymore if you think it's gonna get us caught. But can we watch the tape one last time?"

"And then destroy it?"

"Yes, if you think it might get us caught."

"Don't you?"

"Yeah, you're probably right. Hey, what if I could use everything to throw the cops off our scent? You know, make someone else look guilty?"

"Whatever you come up with, you better do it fast."

"Okay, gimme some time to think it through."

Pleased that she listened to him, he continued, convincing her that they needed to replace the pickup with a car. She gave him three hundred bucks in case he would need some money to close the deal. While she worked on altering her appearance, he drove to a small used car lot a few miles away. He easily traded the pickup for a 1975 cranberry-colored Oldsmobile Cutlass and one hundred fifty dollars. On the way back to the motel, he stopped in a

convenience store and picked up some candy, chips and a six-pack of beer. The cashier was watching the news and Reuben's stomach flipped when pictures of him and Doll side-by-side flashed on the screen. Thank God he shaved. He hastily paid for his purchases and left.

When she opened the door for him, naked, the room reeked with the smell of marijuana. "Noche y Dia", Al B. Sure's Spanish version of "Night and Day" played on the small alarm clock radio. He shut the door, to prevent the smell from leaving the room. Doll sat back on the bed. He couldn't believe how different she looked. She had not only dyed her hair black, she also cut it into a short bob with bangs. The darker hair contrasted against her pale skin and her bloodshot brown eyes seemed smaller. He went to her and grabbed her up in his arms, burying his face in her motel soap-smelling neck, but she had other things on her mind. Doll stopped him by backing away and getting right to the point.

"I've been thinking. We need a fall guy. Someone the police would believe is capable of committing these so-called crimes. Do you have any idea where Miguel is? I think he'd be perfect. Besides, we used his blackjack on Dominic, so that's a good start."

"I don't know. How can we connect them with the stiletto and gun?"

"Okay, let me think. They probably can't trace the knife and if they trace the gun back to me, maybe you could say you took it from me and gave it to him to hold. After all, it would have been a parole violation and you're trying to keep me out of trouble. The only tricky part will be finding Miguel. Then all we have to do is plant the evidence. How 'bout we go visit your mom? If she doesn't know where he

is, maybe we'll find something that'll lead him to us. This way we could kill two birds with one baggie."

Reuben had to admit that if they could pull it off, it sounded like a pretty good idea and he had no qualms about putting Miguel behind bars. He owed him that.

"Okay, I'll be right back. Gonna call my mom." He went outside to the phone booth next to the check-in office.

As soon as his mother heard his voice she excitedly lapsed into Spanish.

"Dios mío, ¿Dónde has estado? ¿Conoce la policía está buscando a ti? Te están diciendo y una niña que han hecho cosas terribles."

"I know, Mama. It's not true. I think someone's trying to frame me.

"¿Quién, que haría eso?"

"That's what I'm trying to find out. Would it be okay if I came by?"

"No sé, hijo, la policía he estado aquí unas par de veces que pregunta por usted. Pueden mirar la casa." Her voice got lower each time she spoke.

"Mamá, Inglés, por favor."

"I think police are watching my house."

Shit, hadn't thought of that. He began thinking about how to adapt his plan.

"Okay, how about I meet you at the Green Acres Mall food court?"

"Reuben, what if the police are listening to our call?"

"I guess it's a chance we'll have to take."

"I don't like taking chances."

You should have thought about that before you brought that molester into our home.

"Mama, please, you've gotta help me fix this."

"I'll meet you there in an hour."

When he hung up, he returned to Doll, pleased with the results. He scribbled some notes on the receipt from the convenience store.

"Here's my old house key," he said as he moved it in a circular motion to remove it from the key ring. "While I meet Mom, I want you to slip into the house and find anything you can that will lead us to Miguel. Use the back door, in fact, go to the corner of the block and cut through the backyards 'til you reach the cocoa brown house with beige shutters. It's the only one with a clothesline in the back.

"I'll try to keep her away for at least an hour. If there is someone watching the house, hopefully they'll follow her when she leaves. I'm gonna stall as long as I can, but you have find something that will lead us to Miguel. Be thorough and be fast. I've mapped out the bus route. The express should get you there in fifteen to twenty minutes. Whether you find anything or not, I want you out of there in forty-five minutes, no more, understand? Then catch the Q85 and meet me at Nathan's. In case the police are following Mom, I'm taking the gun."

He stuck the gun in his waistband, making sure it was in the middle of his back and pulled out his shirttail to keep it hidden. Reuben held out the piece of paper. She stood up and came so close he could feel her nipples burning his chest at their point of contact. Doll took the directions out

of his hand.

♣♣♣

"Look at you, you've got it all figured out," Doll congratulated him. This was the first time he'd taken the initiative and she appreciated it.

"Baby, if we can't pull this off, we're gonna be shit out of luck, you know that, don't you? It's just a matter of time before someone spots us and turns us in."

"Then we need to make the most of the time we have left, don't we?" She slipped the tape in the motel's TV/VCR combo and turned it on. "Come on, baby, one last time, for old time's sake."

As they watched, she slowly slid her hands under his shirt, removed the gun and kissed him, pulling him down on the bed with her.

Chapter Seventeen

THE VARIOUS STATE, county and city law enforcement agencies created a task force of their most talented detectives. Based on Shevaughn's arrest record, they called and asked for her participation. She was excited about the prospect, yet dreaded telling Marcus about it because she knew he would not be pleased.

She'd spoken to Mattie that morning. After leaving the precinct, Shevaughn went home, grabbed the diaper bag and filled it with diapers and bottles of formula. Next, she collected the kids and the dog and took them all to Mattie's house. It would be the first time DJ spent the night away from her and she wondered if six weeks was too early for the separation. Mattie held him and assured her that she had nothing to worry about. Shevaughn broke down and told her about the rift that wouldn't go away between her and Marcus.

"So you're saying he wants you to quit your job?"

"Yeah and if he makes me choose, he's not gonna win. He's trying to control me. I don't know when it started or why I didn't recognize it before. I just don't get how it's become such an issue all of a sudden. You know I've been pretty self-sufficient most of my adult life and I don't do submissive well. Still, I don't want my kids growing up

without their dad. Either way, I lose."

"I wish I could tell you some way to make it all better, but there's no magic wand I can wave to fix it. Someone's got to compromise or someone's got to go," Mattie advised.

"That's what I'm afraid of."

"Look, go home. Make a nice dinner and get pretty. Maybe after a glass of wine or two, you'll figure something out. A little love can smooth out the bumps."

Something tells me it's gonna take a lot more than that.

"Toni, come say goodbye. I'm leaving," Shevaughn called out.

Her daughter came to the door with Q behind her. He stopped about a foot away from them and watched them kiss and hug. Shevaughn recognized the look on his face. *Good Lord, the feeling is mutual!* Toni must have won him over because he now looked at her with matching adoration. Shevaughn shared a hug with Mattie.

"We need to keep an eye on those two," Shevaughn whispered. Mattie nodded.

"I know. Puppy love's adorable, huh?" They hid their laughter from the children.

On the ride home, Shevaughn found herself suffering from so much anxiety that she almost turned the car around to get her son, but she wanted this time with Marcus without any interruptions.

Home again, she went straight to the kitchen and started preparing all her husband's favorites, hoping to soften him up. Once dinner was almost ready, she turned everything off, took a quick shower and chose the black and gold batwing caftan from their closet. He'd bought it for her last

Christmas and just wearing it made her feel regal. She finished it off with a touch of makeup and a light spritz of Obsession. She brushed her hair, which she now wore shorter for convenience, added her black kitten-heel mules and gold door-knocker earrings to complete the picture.

He walked in the front door and the aromas of the smothered pork chops, rice, gravy, collards and cornbread greeted him. Marcus immediately became suspicious. *What is she up to?*

"Hey hon, will you pour us some wine? I'll be right out."

He checked out the bottle of wine in the ice bucket. When he saw it was the '75 Felton Road Riesling they were saving for a special occasion, he was positive that something was up. Then she walked out, not dressed in her usual baggy sweats, but in the caftan he hadn't seen since months before DJ's birth. He tried to think as he handed her a half-filled glass of wine.

"Where are the kids?"

"At Mattie's. I thought we were due for some 'we' time. I even took Kayla over there."

"So it's just you and me?"

"Yes, it's just us."

Suddenly, it clicked. She'd gone for her checkup today. The six-week drought was over! He decided to enjoy this moment with his wife and took a long sip of his wine. From the look of things, she had been anticipating it as much as he had.

"Now I want you to sit down and I'll make your plate."

He'd just tasted his first mouthful of rice and gravy when the phone rang.

Marcus let out a groan.

"Come on, baby, don't answer that."

"You know I have to. It could be Mattie." *Or the precinct.*

When she heard Jared's voice, her heart sunk. She wanted to make sure Marcus was in a mellow mood before she told him about the task force.

"I'll be right there."

"Is it the kids? Is everything okay? Where are you going?"

"Marc, I'm so sorry. That was the precinct, I've gotta go."

"Tell me this isn't happening. Technically, you're not even supposed to go back to work full-time until Monday. Why do you have to go now?"

"We may have a lead on those unsolved murders."

"And no one can handle it but you, right?"

"I'm not saying that, but they made me part of the task force and I *am* gonna be there."

"Okay, Von, I've tried to do things your way. But every time I've had to watch you leave for the precinct, I get that sick feeling in the pit of my stomach, worrying if you'd make it back home alive. Honestly, these last few weeks have been damn near perfect and I want it to stay that way. I want a wife. I can't do this 'you're the big, bad cop' thing anymore. It's not fair to me or the kids. I thought you would see the importance of this after DJ was born, but I guess not. If you leave now, I swear 'fore God, Von, I won't be here when you get back! You got that?" Marcus got up

from the table and stood in her face, shouting. He was furious.

"Yes, Marc," Shevaughn calmly answered. "I think I finally do. You go and do what you have to because that's exactly my intention."

Shevaughn ran to the bedroom, hastily changed from her evening attire into her ivory button front blouse that tied at the neck, beige pantsuit and dark brown loafers. She quickly headed for the door to avoid getting into a real knock-down, dragged-out fight. As she closed it, she thought she heard him say, "You're making a big mistake."

On the ride to the precinct, she couldn't help but think about her situation. As much as she loved Marcus, she now thought that maybe she'd jumped into the marriage too soon. For the first time in years she thought about Tony. He'd been more appreciative and understanding about her job. Her eyes began to burn. She turned on the radio to drown out her feelings only to hear Anita Baker singing and asking for "Good Love" as if she knew exactly how Shevaughn felt.

She turned off the radio and burst into tears. A sharp pain in her chest made her realize that you *can* feel your heart break. Shevaughn pulled over to the side of the road, beat her fist against the steering wheel and let it all out. It took a while for the moment to pass, but when it finally did, she took a deep breath and gave herself a silent pep talk. *Girl, get yourself together. It's not the end of the world. This too shall pass.* She took a tissue out of her purse, dried her tears and checked her reflection in the mirror from her makeup case. Her eyes were red and swollen from crying and she knew she looked terrible. Nevertheless, she pulled

herself together and continued on to the precinct.

When she arrived, the precinct was a frenzy of activity with everyone on high alert. Finally, the surveillance on Reuben's mother's home may have paid off. Hidden, they watched Mrs. Mendoza leave the house and then an unmarked car followed her to the mall. Two plainclothes detectives were keeping her in their sights. There wasn't any sign of Reuben yet, but with any luck...

"Come on, Von, we gotta go."

"Where to?"

"We bugged Mrs. Mendoza phone. She took off for the Green Acres Mall after getting a call from her son. We called the Suffolk County Police Department and they're gonna meet us there."

♣♣♣

Hoping she'd be able to plant the evidence, Doll put the stiletto and baggie in her purse right before she left the motel. She found it hard to destroy the tape, so she hid it in her sanitary pad box. She knew the authorities would never look there.

Doll walked three blocks to the bus stop and arrived at Reuben's mom's house twenty minutes later. Using the key he gave her, she slipped in the back door of a small one-level home. Too small to be considered a ranch, it was the product of a mass-produced suburb.

The home's appearance wasn't as foreign as she expected it to be. In fact, it looked like thousands of lower middle class homes, regardless of the race or color of the occupants. The décor was a little too floral for Doll's tastes, but then again, old Mrs. Mendoza lived alone for a long

time. The house was tiny and neat.

She started her search with the overflowing basket of mail on the living room coffee table. Doll thought it may have been collecting for some time, but after she checked all of the envelopes, she discovered that the oldest postmark was less than six months ago. Reuben said Miguel moved out a month before he was released. She realized what a long-shot this whole search was. Her stomach soured and she felt her body tremble, confirming how nervous this whole ordeal made her. It felt like the time she waited for the supermarket boy to call, except this time, the phrase "a matter of life and death" fit appropriately. Doll hastily rummaged through the kitchen drawers, finding nothing but cutlery, take-out menus, potholders and kitchen towels. *Useless*.

She hurried to the first bedroom which she assumed was Reuben's. Standing in the doorway, she quickly appraised the area. It looked like it hadn't been touched since the police carted Reuben off in handcuffs all those years ago. It appeared to be the room of the typical teenage boy. It had a full-size bed, an Atari 2600 sat on the dresser along with a small TV and several *Mad Max* and *Enter the Dragon* posters hung on the walls. This was a side of him that she didn't know about, but she didn't have time to investigate. She went on. The odds of finding something leading to Miguel in Reuben's room were probably 100 to 1.

Doll hurried to his mom's room. *Geez, more flowers.* Between the wallpaper and the bedspread, it looked like a garden had thrown up in there. She went through the dresser drawers, looked under the mattress and bed, checked out the closet and came up with nothing. Her time was running out and she hadn't accomplished a thing. Panic began to rise and brought a sour taste to the back of

her throat. Doll stood for a moment, took a couple of deep breaths and calmed down through sheer will. *This is a colossal risk and a waste of time.*

For a moment, she thought about leaving the evidence in Reuben's mom's house since she had every intention of playing somebody's victim. She then realized that would be another mistake. If the cops figured out someone else put them there, all fingers, pun intended, would point to her. She knew that somehow she could make them believe that Reuben forced her to be his accomplice. It may be the only way to save her life. With that thought, she decided not to go to the mall. Instead, she headed for the drug store.

Chapter Eighteen

AT FIRST HE didn't see his mother and for a moment he panicked. He went up and down the food court and just when he was ready to give up, he saw her at Sbarro's. Relief swept over him and he rushed to her side.

"Mama, thanks for coming."

"No, don't thank me. Hijo, the police are saying you've done some terrible things. Tell me it's not true."

"It isn't, Mom, I swear."

"Then why would they say such things?"

"I don't know, Mom. I guess they need someone to pin the blame on. That's why I have to get out of here."

"I think you should turn yourself in, get this straightened out."

"I can't until I know what's happening and what they think they have on me. Mom, did you bring any money? It's just a loan. If you can go pick up my paycheck, I'll sign it over to you."

"The police are probably watching your job, too. Just pay me back after you get this fixed, but I will need my money back." She tapped her purse for emphasis.

"I promise I will."

"In the meantime, you need to stay hidden. Here's seventy-five dollars. I know it's not much."

"That's the best you could do?"

"On such short notice, yes. I'm trying to help. I still think you'd be better off going to the police."

"I can't, Mom. Trust me. I'm gonna figure a way out of this."

"You better do it fast."

"I know. You think I like being in this situation?"

They were so intent on their conversation that they didn't notice the small group of people slowly moving into their proximity. When they did, it was too late.

As the police closed in on the couple, it was obvious that Reuben and his mother knew that they were caught. They looked around for an avenue of escape. Shevaughn took a closer look at the boy. She knew he had just turned twenty-two, yet he could have easily passed for eighteen, although that's not the way it's typically done. Usually teenagers try to pass themselves off as older. *My God, he's just a kid!* When she thought about the body count and the manner in which the victims died, it was hard to imagine him capable of such cruelty.

Reuben pulled the gun from his waistband.

Everybody stopped. Shevaughn looked at the boy and noticed a slight tremble. Instinctively, she took a small step closer to him, speaking softly. She remained empty-handed with both of her hands positioned in front of her with her palms down.

"Okay, Reuben, let's not do anything rash. You need to hand me the gun. I know you didn't expect it to come to this. But it must have dawned on you that this wasn't a game, that you were making choices that would destroy your life forever."

"Don't listen to her, Mom. She doesn't know what she's talking about." Reuben yelled.

Shevaughn continued, "Where is she, Reuben? I know this isn't what you wanted. You just wanted her to love you, wanted to keep her with you. You did anything she asked as long as it made her happy. She used that against you and took you down this dark road. That's not love. You do know that, don't you?"

♣♣♣

Shevaughn felt his decision before she saw it. He looked at his mom, moved away and raised the gun. His intention was clear and they all reacted. It happened in a blink of an eye.

"Gun! Everybody down!" a voice yelled. Shevaughn thought it might have been Jared. She watched as a bullet caught Reuben in the shoulder and spun him around. Even though Reuben had been shot, he still didn't drop the gun.

He looked Shevaughn dead in the eye and pointed the pistol in the direction of the police officers. Suddenly, it sounded like the Fourth of July. There were firecrackers everywhere. Only after he sank to his knees did he realize that the sound was the barrage of gunfire. They were killing him. Bleeding out, he saw the shock and grief on his mother's face and felt a moment of immense regret.

"Hold your fire," Shevaughn yelled, but they all knew it was too late.

"WHY?" Mrs. Mendoza screamed and ran to her son. Crying, she knelt beside him and cradled his body against her breast, rocking him like she had hundreds of times before, long ago when he was a child.

Chapter Nineteen

DOLL RETURNED TO the drugstore, but the girl who'd caught her attention had already left. Hungry, she decided to go to the small, non-descript restaurant located in the strip mall across the street from their motel. She ordered meatloaf, mashed potatoes and a side salad. Surprisingly, it tasted like a home-cooked meal. Full, she returned to the motel and waited for Reuben.

She turned on the TV and reclined on the bed. A newsflash interrupted *21 Jump Street*:

"The search for two murder suspects came to a deadly end for one of them late this afternoon when suspected rapist and murderer Reuben Armando Mendoza was fatally shot at the Green Acres Mall. Mendoza is suspected in the murders of at least five people. The police are still searching for his alleged accomplice, Dahlia McMillan Henderson. If you have any information regarding the whereabouts of Dahlia McMillan Henderson, please call 212-567-TIPS."

Her mug shot from eight years ago flashed across the screen. She felt a little more confident when she realized that she looked nothing like that now.

They'd killed Reuben. She wanted to feel grief, but, *that's what happens when someone else does the planning.* She

finished her joint from the morning while she checked her stash. Doll had a dime of weed, a little 'Special K' and three 300-milligram Quaalude tablets left. She held on to the 'ludes for a special occasion. Her number-one concerns were to get more cash, to get a car and to leave this place. It felt as the motel walls were closing in on her and she wondered if she could suddenly develop claustrophobia. If she could somehow trade places with the drugstore cashier, it might answer all of her prayers.

As she watched the suspect die in his mother's arms, Shevaughn wondered where Dahlia Henderson could be hiding. After the attendants removed Reuben from the mall floor and placed his body in the ambulance, the police searched the mall and checked the security tapes from the cameras in the food court. No one resembling Dahlia came to the mall today. Shevaughn believed that although Reuben may have been a willing participant, Dahlia called the shots. Until they apprehended her, the case wouldn't be closed.

She left the mall, stopped at Mattie's and picked the kids up early. She didn't want to go back to her empty home.

"So it didn't go well?" Mattie asked. Shevaughn shook her head "no".

"Hell, Mattie, it didn't go at all. We'd just started eating when the precinct called. He said if I left, he'd be gone when I got back, so I'm expecting to go home to an empty house." She fought back the tears. They packed up the kids and she could tell Toni was quite upset with her.

"Why do we have to leave, Mommy? I thought I was spending the night!"

"I'm sorry, but I missed you and DJ too much. You can spend the night another time, I promise. I just wanted you with me. Don't worry, everything's gonna be okay."

"No, it's not. Auntie Real says she's getting away with it."

"Who is?"

"The flower girl." *Was Toni talking about Dahlia? How would she know?*

"She says it's not over." Shevaughn shivered as she remembered Ariel saying the exact same thing at Tony's funeral. She had been so right then and Shevaughn had a feeling she would be again.

"What else did she say?"

"The flower girl is leaving and going far away."

"Did she say where?"

"No, but..." Toni looked a little uncomfortable about relaying the rest of Ariel's message.

"But what, honey? You can tell me."

"She said it's hot as Hell."

"Toni!"

"Well, you asked. She said it, not me."

"Okay, but I don't want to hear that from you again, understand?"

"Yes, Mom, I knew it would get me in trouble."

When they arrived home, she was surprised to see Marcus still there. He'd eaten dinner and finished the bottle of wine, alone. Shevaughn tried to eat, but her stomach wouldn't cooperate. In front of Toni, both

pretended everything was okay, but they all felt the undercurrent of tension. After giving Marcus a quick good night hug, Toni went up to her room and closed the door to avoid hearing any of the confrontation. *She's probably pulling out "Mother Crocodile" again.*

"She knows something's wrong."

"I can't argue with that."

"Marc, we can work this out."

"How? You've clearly shown me your job is your priority. It's more important to you than your family. I keep trying to make it right, but it's like trying to dig my way to China. No matter how much progress I make, it'll never happen. That's why I'm moving out this weekend. I give up. You'll be hearing from my lawyer next week to discuss support and visitation."

"Whatever man, do what you feel. You could have done us all a favor and been gone when we got back, like you said." Shevaughn put the leftovers away and went to her room.

Later that night, Shevaughn retired to the bedroom while Marcus slept on the futon in the den. She was awakened by the sound of Toni's screams, immediately followed by DJ's frightened cries. Shevaughn ran to Toni's room and turned on the light. Toni was sitting up in bed with tears streaming down her face. Shevaughn sat down and held her, feeling her little body tremble in her arms.

"Mommy, you need to go to Nonna's, NOW."

"What is it, Hon? Did you have a bad dream?"

"Hurry, before it's too late."

"It's late, honey, can't I just call her?"

"Nooooo, Mommy, please. Go right now. Something's wrong. And don't ring the doorbell. Bang on the door. Promise you won't ring the bell."

Toni was so agitated, Shevaughn decided to humor her. Marcus left the den, checked on Lil' D and came to Toni's room. He stayed with her while Shevaughn jumped in the car and took off for Nonna's. Her daughter's late night demands frightened her and although she wouldn't usually do it for a personal matter, she turned on her patrol car's siren and flashing lights. Shevaughn sped all the way to her destination and banged on the front door like Toni begged her to.

Nonna answered the door, coughing. Speaking, her voice sounded raspy.

"Von, how did you know?"

"Know what?"

"The house smells of gas. I thought I accidently left one of the burners on. I woke up choking and was trying to open some of the windows and here you are!"

"Come outside with me and get some fresh air," Shevaughn instructed as she grabbed Nonna around the shoulders and led her outdoors. She made her sit down on the stoop. "I'll go check the gas."

She returned a couple of minutes later.

"Really, why are you here?" Nonna asked again.

"Okay, you might not believe this, but I think Ariel has been talking to Toni and warned her about the gas. She was very insistent that I come over here immediately and made me promise not to call or ring the bell. It's like she knew it could set off an explosion."

"I believe you. You know what woke me up? I could swear I heard Ariel yelling in my ear to get out of the house. I went to the kitchen and figured out the pilot light had gone out, but I didn't know for how long, so I was afraid to light it. I opened some windows and walked to the front door when you knocked. Something told me not to turn on the light. Thank God there's a full moon tonight, so I didn't need it. You know, I always believed the spirits of loved ones watch over us and now I think we have our own personal guardian angel. She's making sure we stay safe, isn't she?"

The thought brought Shevaughn comfort.

"I lit the pilot light. Let's get someone from the gas company come over in the morning and check it. I'd feel better if you came home with me tonight."

"Okay, I'll go with you.

They went back into the house and with all the windows open, they could barely smell the gas. Shevaughn made sure all the windows were closed and locked while Nonna threw a few things in a small bag. Then they got into Shevaughn's Volvo and headed home.

She thought she should mention what was happening before they got there.

"The den's occupied, but there's a daybed in the nursery."

"So what are you saying? Marcus is sleeping in the den? Is it that bad?"

"Oh Nonna, it's even worse."

Shevaughn opened up and told Nonna about her day, Marcus, his control issues and the end of her marriage.

Chapter Twenty

DOLL WENT TO the drugstore that Monday afternoon and started up a conversation with the cashier. That's when she learned she worked late on Wednesdays. *Perfect*.

"We could be sisters," Doll proclaimed after they introduced themselves. They laughed at their resemblance, especially now that she'd changed her hair color. She gave Jamie the story of being new in town and not knowing anyone. "You're my first friend in this boring town." They made plans to meet Wednesday after work. Jamie promised to take her to a couple of bars in town.

Wednesday afternoon, Doll bought a bottle of strawberry Cisco, figuring that even though the Quaaludes were almost tasteless, the strong drink would make it impossible to detect. After rolling a joint in preparation, she used the stiletto to crush the three 'ludes and dropped the powder in the bottom of Jamie's Dixie cup. Afterwards, she filled it with the strong-tasting drink, stirred it and placed it in the freezer next to her baggie.

Doll showed up a few minutes before Jamie was supposed to get off from work. She suggested they stop by her motel room in order to get a head start on their high before they hit the clubs. Jamie agreed and drove them back to the motel. Doll gave her the cold drink and lit the

joint. When Jamie tried to pass it back to her, she refused after a couple of hits. She wanted to keep a clear head and only took a sip from her cup so Jamie wouldn't get suspicious. They sat on the motel bed and Jamie got toasted.

"Woo, that really hit me hard," Jamie commented as she finished her second cup of Cisco. I gotta lie down for a minute," she mumbled, rubbing her forehead.

"Sure, go ahead. It's a little early anyway."

"I feel so weird."

"It's okay, I'll lay down with you and we can take a catnap. I bet we'll both feel better in a little while. People warned me about that Cisco. Heard they call it liquid crack. I should have listened." She got extra pillows from the closet and gave them both to Jamie.

She waited and watched Jamie doze off, laying on her side. When she was sure the drugs were doing their job and Jamie was out of it, Doll got up from the bed, took the black jack from her purse and hit her in the back of the head to make sure she was totally unconscious. She rolled Jamie on her back, got undressed and slid on top of her. When she felt no resistance, she slipped her tongue into Jamie's mouth. It almost felt like she was making love to herself. Doll unbuttoned Jamie's blouse and pulled up her bra, allowing herself the pleasure of sampling her larger breasts. She slid further down, pulling Jamie's panties with her and stuck her tongue into Jamie as far as she could. She stopped to position Jamie's butt on the pillows, raising her closer. Her lack of reaction strangely turned Doll on. She finished removing Jamie's clothes and put them on the chair next to her suitcase.

Crawling between her legs, Doll enjoyed her sweet, musty taste and masturbated into an orgasm. After she came, she crawled up until she knelt on Jamie's shoulders, wrapped her hands around her throat and pressed down on her windpipe. She went so far as to jump up and down on her knees to put as much weight as possible on her throat. It felt surreal, like she was choking herself in a mirror. *Mirror!* She went back to her purse for her makeup mirror and the stiletto. When she saw the fog of Jamie's breath on the mirror, Doll stabbed her exactly a dozen times. She counted each thrust and made sure at least two of them were life threatening. Blood spattered everywhere, but at least now she knew the bitch wasn't breathing.

Exhausted, Doll went into the bathroom, took a shower and changed into a nondescript heather gray sweat suit she'd bought at Kmart. She sat in the motel chair and searched through Jamie's purse, switched their wallets and then took the keys, singling out the one for her car. Doll went outside, opened the trunk of the blue two-door 1980 Buick Regal, found the jack and took the removable handle back into the room with her. She rapidly stepped out of her clothes. When completely naked, Doll stood over what used to be Jamie. Using all her strength, she raised the handle over her head with both arms, swung down as hard as she could and proceeded to bash Jamie's skull in until exhaustion prevented her from raising her arms anymore.

When she was positive that no one could recognize her, she got the cigar cutter and snipped away. She didn't add Jamie's fingertips to the baggie, because if the bag was found, the police would find out that Jamie wasn't Doll. Instead, she put them in an empty potato chip bag with the intention of dropping them along her route. After a speedy shower to wash the blood off a second time, she changed

into Jamie's clothes. They fit a little big on her, but she fixed that problem by tying the shirt bottom around her waist. Before she left, Doll turned the thermostat up as high as it would go, hoping the heat would make it hard to determine the time of death. She thought she remembered reading that somewhere. She left the motel, got into Jamie's car and started it up. She made a U-turn and headed west toward I-495. She stopped at a Safeway gas station and filled up using Jamie's credit card. *Time to start my new life.*

As Doll entered Missouri on I-70 West, she stopped at the next truck stop she saw, pulled in and told the story of how her boyfriend got shot down right before her very eyes to any man who would listen. Men were always sympathetic to petite, pretty young things. This resulted in a lot of "comforting". Some guys comfort with liquor or drugs, others with sex, some with both. She took whatever they had to offer and didn't leave until late the following evening. Then her mourning period ended as swiftly as it began and she got back on the road.

Chapter Twenty-One

THE FOLLOWING SATURDAY morning, Kennedy stood at the kitchen sink and waited until she heard Jared's car pull out of the driveway. Today she would get to the bottom of this. One Saturday a month, almost like clockwork, he left on the pretense of going to a hardware or auto store, knowing she wouldn't want to go. A few times he came home empty-handed with a funny look on his face. Kennedy knew he was hiding something. She may not be a detective, but she wasn't stupid either. She would follow him today and see if he went anywhere else other than hardware store.

She jumped in her car and caught a glimpse of him stopping at the light. When she expected him to turn left into the Ace hardware store parking lot, he surprised her by passing the entrance and continuing down the street. *Where is he going?* She knew she had to be cautious, after all she was following a cop. Yet that didn't stop her. She had to know. She followed him from as far behind as she could without losing sight of his car.

When he pulled into a parking space in front of a red brick apartment building, she stopped short and looked for somewhere to park so she could watch him. Kennedy hurriedly parked near the complex exit and got out of the car just in time to see what looked like him opening the

lobby door with a key. The phrase "double life" popped into her head and for the first time, she thought her man was cheating on her.

She intended to wait until he left to confront him, but her curiosity got the best of her. After a few minutes, which seemed like forever to her, she followed her husband. When she couldn't enter the lobby door, she hit every button on the building's security panel, hoping someone would let her in. The sound of the answering buzzer relieved and scared her at the same time. She slipped inside the doorway and wondered how she would find him when she heard his laughter through the paper-thin walls. She followed the sound, walked down the hall past two apartment doors and knocked on the third.

When a woman answered the door, it felt like someone kicked her in the stomach. Her tall, sexy, milk chocolate-complexioned husband stood behind a stranger with a child in his arms. Looking at the three of them, Kennedy fought down the nausea in her throat and held onto the door jamb to steady herself.

"What the fuck is going on, Jared? And who the hell is this bitch?"

Jared's life flashed before his eyes and his first thought was to lie…and run. *How the hell did she find me?* He handed the toddler to the woman as he rushed to the door.

"Kennedy, what are you doing here?"

"I could ask you the same question."

"It's not what you think."

"What do I think? I think that you have some woman in

your little fuck nest and that you've been lying and keeping secrets from me. Whose kid is that?" She stopped and looked closely at the boy, examining his features.

"Oh...good Lord, no...it's yours, isn't it? Never mind, I can see that for myself. So what does that make me, your personal village idiot?"

"No, I swear it's not like that. This all happened before we even met. We only slept together once and I didn't even know she was pregnant 'til after the baby was born. Tell her, Lori."

He looked to the mother of his child for help, but Kennedy stepped around her as if she didn't exist and didn't let Lori get a word in edgewise.

"I don't want to hear it from her, Jared. I want to hear it from you. You're supposed to be the man. If this was such an 'accident', why didn't you tell me all about it when we met? You knew by then, didn't you?"

"No, wait, I didn't know about him 'til after we met. I wanted to tell you, I just couldn't figure out the right words or the right time...and the next thing I knew it was too late."

"It's never too late to tell the truth. How 'bout before you went on one of your so-called hardware store trips? You could've said, 'Oh yeah, babe and on the way home I'm making a stop to see my son. Would you like to meet him?'"

"Okay, it couldn't happen like that. We were so happy...Well, until you started pressuring me for a kid. Then it was even harder to come clean. I know I was wrong, but you gotta know I didn't plan to hurt you."

"Now it's all starting to make sense. Is that why you were so adamant on handling our finances? Maybe so I wouldn't see that you were sending her money? I understand why you didn't want us to have a child right away. What, you didn't think you could afford two kids? And what am I supposed to do now? Forgive and forget? That's expecting a little much, don't you think? How could you, Jared? How could you do this to us? "

Kennedy broke and a deep sob escaped her lips. He stepped closer to her and in an attempt to comfort her, he gently touched her shoulder. His touch sparked her anger even more.

"Get away from me, Jared!" She screamed, jerking her body away. "What a fool I am. When Marcus moved back in with Mom and Dad, I felt sorry for my brother because of his marital problems. I actually thanked God for what we have. Now I find out I don't have shit!"

"Yes, you do," Lori spoke for the first time. "You have a good man. We didn't mean for this to happen, but when he found out, he stepped up and accepted his responsibility. A lot of guys would have disappeared, but not your husband. And he's telling you the truth, it only happened once and he ended it before he met you."

Kennedy didn't know what to believe. She needed time to think. *I have to get out of here.*

"Can we…" Jared began.

"No…*we*…can't…do…shit," she said slowly, tilting her head side-to-side in order to emphasize each word. She wiped her nose on her sleeve. "I've gotta get out of here and get myself together and I can't do it with you up in my

face." She looked from Jared to Lori and then to the little boy. Before she left, she needed to ask just one more question. She had to know.

"What's his name?"

"Jared Junior," Lori answered.

They'd even stolen her future son's name. That was the final straw.

Kennedy didn't remember leaving the apartment or getting into her car. Her mind was filled with thoughts of betrayal and the loss of trust. She doubted that she could ever believe in him again.

She reached for the glove compartment to get a tissue for her eyes and she drove through the yellow light with a little added pressure on the accelerator making sure she made it through the intersection before it turned red. Suddenly appearing out of nowhere, a blue 1980 Vanagon Westfalia T-boned the driver side of her silver 1988 Pontiac Fiero. The car spun around and the sound of screeching tires filled Kennedy's ears just before her world faded to black.

Chapter Twenty-Two

KENNEDY WOKE UP to the bright white of the hospital lights and a sea of concerned faces. She tried to speak and found her mouth so dry that her tongue seemed glued to its roof.

"She's awake." She recognized her dad's voice and turned her head in his direction. "Welcome back, baby girl."

Her immediate family stood at her bedside and she gazed, puzzled at the worry on their faces. She saw Mom and Dad, Marcus and Shevaughn...and Jared.

"Get him out of here."

Although the words were screaming in her head, they came out as a dry whisper. Everyone turned to stare at Jared and a hurt look crossed his face. She felt a little satisfaction for putting it there. He left the room without saying a word.

"Are you thirsty?" Her mother held a small plastic cup. She picked up a few ice chips and put them on her tongue. It felt good.

"What happened?" Kennedy whispered. The last thing she remembered was hearing the boy's name.

"You were in a car accident and scared the hell out of us.

You've been unconscious for the last four hours, but now you're going to be fine. The doctor said you have a bruised back, concussion and your right arm and leg are fractured." Kennedy looked down and saw her arm in a cast. She wiggled her toes, or at least she thought she did.

If Jared thought he felt guilty before, it wasn't even close to what he felt now. He would have given anything to go back in time, back to before she knew. Hell, if he could only go back to before "tequila night", as he called it. He wanted to kick his own ass for getting into this mess, yet if that meant giving up his son, he knew he couldn't do that. He refused to be that statistical absentee father. His son would know who he was, even though he wasn't proud of what he'd done.

As he walked towards the hospital exit, he was stopped by a doctor.

"Mr. Benjamin?"

"Detective Benjamin," he corrected and flashed his badge.

"Yes, Detective Benjamin, I'm Dr. Rico Jordan. Has anyone explained the extent of your wife's injuries?"

"She has a broken arm and leg and a concussion?"

"I'm afraid it's more serious than that. Can you come to my office so we can talk?"

"Sure, Doc. Lead the way."

Together, they walked to the end of the hall and got into the elevator. They rode in silence while Jared tried to think of a way to start the conversation. On second thought, he wasn't in a rush. Something told him he really didn't want

to hear what the doctor had to say.

They got off on the third floor and walked down the long, antiseptic-smelling hall. Dr. Jordan opened his door, ushered Jared in and offered him a seat.

He sat behind his desk and reached for a file from his inbox.

"As I said, your wife's condition is critical. You didn't notice the body cast? She suffered an injury to the vertebrae in her lumbar region and it pinched her spinal cord. I'm afraid she has suffered what we refer to as an incomplete spinal cord injury. We performed surgery to correct the vertebrae misalignment and we have her on methylprednisolone to reduce the cord inflammation. Right now, all we can do is wait and see how it plays out. We'll test her reactions to stimulus several times a day and monitor her pain. Worst-case scenario, she has a 50/50 chance of paralysis. However, some patients have been known to make a complete recovery with physical therapy, time and patience. The fact that the injury is in her lower lumbar region is in her favor. There are more cases of patients recovering the use of their legs."

"Wait, what…paralysis? Are you saying she won't be able to walk? She'll be a paraplegic?" He hadn't known the depths of his guilt until that very moment. His life seemed to be ruled by a series of accidents; first the hit and run when he met Lori, then accidently getting her pregnant and now a car accident could rob Kennedy of her ability to walk.

"Like I said, Detective Benjamin, we can only wait and see. In the meantime, your wife is going to need your total support."

Yeah, but will she want it? Jared asked himself.

"Well, I appreciate you being straight with me, Doc." They shook hands and Jared left the hospital.

He drove around aimlessly for hours. He couldn't go home, where the ghosts of happier times were lurking in every corner, so he went by the precinct. Maybe if he concentrated on police work he'd get his mind off his current situation. As soon as he got to his desk, he grabbed the Mendoza file and began reading it again. Maybe he'd missed something the first dozen times he read it. As he perused the folder's contents, Shevaughn walked in.

"Hey partner, guess we both had the same idea. A little overtime can't hurt," Shevaughn assumed he wanted extra hours to help with Kennedy's medical bills. She gave him a hug. When they parted, Jared said, "I need to keep busy. I just left the hospital, had a talk with Kennedy's doctor. Her condition is a lot more serious than her parents led us to believe." He explained the events that led up to Kennedy's accident and what the doctor told him. "I want to be there for her, but she ordered me out of her hospital room as soon as she came to."

"Oh my God, Jared, I had no idea. I'm so sorry. You know that if I can do anything for you, just ask, right?"

"Thanks, Von. We could start our own chapter of 'Parents without Partners', huh?" He put his hand on her shoulder. "And Von, I'm sorry. I didn't mean to let blow the whistle on you.

"I know that. Look, don't worry about me. You have enough things on your mind."

"Now that's easier said than done. It's not a fun time for either of us."

"Ain't that the truth?"

"You know I feel partly responsible for you and Marcus separating. He would have never known about your trip to the morgue if I hadn't fucked up."

"You didn't know and you weren't. He wanted to change me and I couldn't let him. I know who I am and I thought he did too. Guess I made a mistake." *That's exactly what Ariel told Toni.*

Shevaughn realized that all of the things Ariel supposedly told Toni were coming true. *What had she said about the "flower girl"? She's getting away with it and it's not over. Who else could she have been referring to other than Dahlia Henderson? And now Jared drops this huge bomb! I had no idea…a son?*

The phone interrupted her thoughts. She heard Jared say, "We're on our way," and Shevaughn grabbed her navy blazer.

"What's up?" She asked as she put her arm in the sleeve.

"They think they found the body of Dahlia Henderson in a motel on the edge of town."

"I'm right behind you."

When they arrived at the motel, a crowd of over thirty people were already milling around. The mob included members of the city, county, state and federal law-enforcement agencies, reporters and curious onlookers. Looking at their faces, it was obvious who had and had not witnessed the crime scene from their expressions and from

the gray pallor that showed on some people's skin.

Shevaughn saw Dr. Spencer speaking with another member of the medical examiner's office and rushed to his side.

"What 'cha got?"

"This was a savage, brutal beating, but that's not what killed her. She's been choked, stabbed probably ten to fifteen times and then someone bashed in her skull with a jack handle that they left on the scene. We're a little unsure as to the time of death because the thermostat had been set as high as it could possibly go. With the room being completely closed, it reached over 100 degrees in there. It's gonna take a little time to pinpoint the actual time of death, but I should be able to give you my educated guess by Monday morning. We also found what we assume are the missing fingertips from prior victims. They were in a baggie by the body. Right now, it looks like Mendoza killed her before meeting his mom at the mall to get help to leave the state. This just might be the end of the case."

Remembering Toni's message from Ariel, Shevaughn wondered if the "hot as hell" comment referred to the motel room temperature. She doubted the case was over, but didn't want to tell the good doctor that this time he might be wrong.

She put on her gloves, walked into the hotel room and immediately felt ill. While most of the crew concentrated on the bed and surrounding area, Shevaughn walked around, looking in drawers and then went to the closet. She spotted a duffle bag, opened it and saw that it contained men's clothes and not Ms. Henderson's as she had expected. *If Reuben killed Dahlia before meeting his Mom and going on the run, why are his clothes still here?* She found a

box of sanitary pads and picked it up to move it out of the way when she heard the rattle of a hard object against the cardboard. Looking inside, she found a VHS tape. She quickly popped it into the motel's VCR and saw the image of Dahlia castrating Mr. Moss. Rewinding the tape to the beginning, all eyes watched Dahlia McMillan Henderson perform a rather enticing strip tease. What followed next haunted them all for a long time.

Chapter Twenty-Three

THEY COLLECTED THE copious amounts of evidence and took notes, photos and samples from every surface. Whoever committed this murder was past the point of caring about leaving evidence. It was hard to believe that all the blood at the crime scene came from such a small girl. The savagery was so apparent to everyone that they couldn't stop themselves from imagining the torture she'd gone. When they were finished, everyone felt drained physically, mentally and emotionally. They all did what came naturally and proceeded to whatever destination housed their next step; be it the lab, morgue, behind a desk filling out an incident report or getting their story together for tonight's news. They all worked until there was nothing left to do but wait for the results that would start coming in as early as tomorrow.

Shevaughn left before Jared.

"Man, I'm whooped. I'm going home and kissing my kids. Are you going back to the hospital?"

For an instant, he wished they could trade places. He really had nowhere to go.

"No, I'm gonna give her some time. Dr. Rico, who's in charge of her case, keeps me informed. What really kicks me in the gut is she needs me now more than ever and she

can't stand the sight of me." He hated when his voice broke. Shevaughn walked to him, gave him a hug and a quick peck on the cheek.

"You can always come hang with us for a while. You know, Toni would love it."

"Nawh, I'll go home in a little while. I just want to look through all the Mendoza files before I leave, then get a fresh start in the morning."

After she left, he read the files and found a similarity between today's murder scene and the Moss case. Both times, someone turned up the thermostat before leaving. He figured it was done to throw off the time of death. He wondered why that seemed to be important. Lost in thought, the next thing he knew, he woke up at his desk. Jared got himself together and went to his car. Without realizing it, he ended up parked outside Lori's apartment. He didn't want to make his problems bigger, but seeing his son would be the only thing that could lift his spirits right now. The prospect of just watching him sleep made him feel better.

When Lori looked through the peephole and saw Jared standing there, she closed her eyes and mouthed the words "thank you". She knew he was standing on her doorstep because he needed them. The day after the accident, he had called her and explained why he might not make his next visit.

"I'm so sorry. If there's anything I can do…" *Obviously, there was.*

She opened the door and let him in, hiding the smile and the warm feeling she felt inside. She'd been waiting for this

night for over a year, telling herself to be patient. She lived for the day that he would finally recognize what he had and from the looks of things, her patience could finally be paying off. Then he spoke and ruined the illusion.

"Lori, I need to talk with you about Kennedy. I know you're still in nursing school, but I wondered, when she comes home from the hospital, how would you feel about moving in with us? This way, we'd all be together, taking care of each other. I could watch our son grow up and you could help me take care of her."

He's gotta be kidding me! There was no way she wanted to be around to watch the two of them. Then again, if she *was* there, maybe she could plant a wedge between them and be there to pick up the pieces when things fell apart.

"Come in, Jared. I've gotta tell you, my first instinct is to tell you no, but I'll listen. Convince me this would be best for all involved, including me. I'm curious to hear what you have to say."

The fact that she didn't immediately shoot down his idea encouraged Jared to continue. Maybe they could figure out a way so that he could have his wife and son under one roof.

Chapter Twenty-Four

SHEVAUGHN STOOD IN the doorway of the living room and watched Nonna sleep on the couch with the TV remote clutched in her hand. When she tried to remove it, the old lady woke up and fiercely snatched it back. Her reflexes were still top-notch. They both laughed.

"Oh Nonna, I needed that!" Shevaughn giggled. She sat down beside her. It felt good to feel Nonna's arm around her shoulders.

"Von, I've been thinking. What would you say to me selling my house and moving in here? That way, I'd always be here for you and the kids. And then they wouldn't have to be uprooted and moved again. Besides, then I could help with expenses, you know, in case of an emergency. Don't answer just yet, Von. Think about it for a while."

"I don't have to. If you want to move in, we can turn the den back into a bedroom. I'd love to have you here." She was grateful for the unexpected offer.

"Well, let's start making arrangements in the morning. You need to go get some sleep."

She was on her way to her room when the phone rang. *Who's calling at this hour?* Somehow, she already knew. When she heard his voice, she hated how it made her feel.

He didn't even say hello and got right down to business.

"Sorry it's so late, but I wanted to catch you when you were home from work. I figured you're probably keeping long hours now that I'm not there." *He couldn't resist the dig.*

"I was just going to bed, Marc, so make it quick."

"So much for being polite, huh? Never mind, I just want to come get the kids this weekend. I miss them...I miss you."

She didn't repeat his sentiment because she refused to give him the satisfaction.

"That's pretty much the price of a separation. Can you pick them up Saturday morning and bring them back Sunday evening?"

"Will you be home?"

"Probably. Good night, Marc."

"Night, Von." She half-expected to hear him end the conversation with "I love you" and felt relief when he didn't.

♣♣♣

Shevaughn said her prayers and got into bed. For the first time since Ariel's death, she whispered a one-sided conversation.

"Okay, so it looks like I could use your help. It's not her, is it? And if it isn't her, then whose body did we find in the motel? Where is Dahlia?" She waited and then realized she didn't know what she was waiting for. She should have gotten more details from Toni. She laughed at herself, turned the light off and was asleep within minutes...

Shevaughn felt the mattress move as if someone sat

down next to her. She opened one eye and thought she saw a vague shadow perched on the corner of the bed by her feet.

"Ariel, is that really you?" she whispered.

"Sure ain't the tooth fairy."

"Shoot, I forgot to put the quarter under Toni's pillow. She lost a tooth this morning."

"See, it's good to have your own guardian angel. How've you been?

"Not too good, but you know that."

"Yes, especially since you've never called on me before. Don't let Marcus get the best of you, you have more important things to worry about. The girl they found today is not the one you're looking for. You need to find her. Don't give up. She's headed west. You'd think of a desert, but there's a lake."

"You know I have no jurisdiction outside of Portsborough. And why are you talking in riddles? Toni said you told her it was hot as hell. Wait, she's near a lake?"

"I'm telling you what I can, how I can. Yes, there's water near, but you wouldn't expect it to be. And if you can't go to her, then make her come to you because if she doesn't, she'll continue leaving bodies wherever she goes. She enjoys the kill. You've got to stop her."

"If she thinks she's gotten away with murder, why would she come back?"

"Appeal to her narcissism and her greed. She can't resist. Trust me."

Shevaughn started to say, "You know I do", when the shadow disappeared.

Turning on the light, she looked around the room. Shevaughn was alone.

She thought about what Ariel said. "You'd think desert." *Okay, so like Arizona, California, New Mexico or Nevada, but don't they all have lakes?* She was going to have to figure out a way to shrink the search area and come up with something a little more specific. Or she could do as Ariel instructed and get Dahlia to return to Portsborough? With that question on her mind, she turned off the light and tried to get some sleep.

As soon as she started to doze back off, she heard a light knock on her bedroom door.

"Come in."

Toni stuck her head in the door. "Mommy, can me and Kayla sleep with you?"

"That's Kayla and I. Why? What's the matter?"

"Nothing, I just thought you might be lonely."

"You know what? I am...a little. You can come on up here, but Kayla gets the rug." Shevaughn nodded at the three-by-five-foot blue, green and brown rag rug that lay on the floor at the end of her bed.

"She won't mind."

Toni walked to the edge of the rug.

"Kayla, down."

The small dog circled the rug a couple of times before lying down and getting comfortable. She stretched her

paws out in front of her. Toni climbed into Shevaughn's bed and snuggled within her arms.

"Mommy, do you think the tooth fairy will know I'm in here with you?"

"Yes, Lil' Bit."

"Good, I need the money for Christmas. Can we invite Miss Mattie and her family to dinner tomorrow?

Cagey little devil, she means Q.

"Sure we can. I'll call her in the morning."

"Know what I want for dinner?"

"What?"

"Chicken and dumplings. We haven't had that in a long time."

Marcus didn't like chicken and dumplings, so she hadn't made one of her favorite dishes since before they'd married and her daughter hadn't crawled into bed with her since the wedding. Shevaughn thought Toni asked to show her, in her own way, that life without Marcus wouldn't be all that bad.

"Okay, chicken and dumplings, it is. Now, good night, Sweet Tea. Love you."

"Love you too. Night, Mommy."

All three of them were softly snoring in no time.

Chapter Twenty-Five

SHEVAUGHN AWOKE AND instantly remembered Ariel's nocturnal visit. She tried to dismiss it by convincing herself it was just a dream, yet it seemed so real. She had a hard time brushing her doubts aside as she started to get ready for work. Having Nonna there to help her with the children in the morning allowed Shevaughn to get to the precinct early, yet when she got to her desk, Dr. Spencer was already there, waiting. And she thought she knew why.

"It's not Dahlia Henderson, is it?"

"What? How did you know? We just discovered the blood types of Ms. Henderson and the woman we found yesterday don't match."

"Call it women's intuition." *She couldn't tell him that Ariel clued her in.* "I think she wanted us to believe that Mendoza murdered her and then went to the mall to meet his mom, but she's really the one behind all these deaths. Did you see the tape?"

"No, but I heard about it."

"She's the leader and he followed. She's probably out there right now searching for somebody else to take his place."

"She's out there somewhere, Von. Something tells me we haven't seen the last of her dirty work."

"I hate to say it, but you're probably right." *At least, that's what Ariel thinks.*

Jared walked in on the conversation.

"Right about what?"

"That the woman we found yesterday wasn't Dahlia Henderson," Dr. Spencer shrugged, as if to say, 'Don't blame me, there's nothing I can do about it'.

"You gotta be kidding me."

"No, she did it to throw us off track, but we haven't given up and closed the case like she thought we would."

"Okay, so our next move is?" Jared looked between Dr. Spencer and Shevaughn. After last night, Jared's mind wasn't on his job. Shevaughn didn't know it, but he was relieved now that she'd taken back the reins.

"I think it's time we set up state border checks, road blocks. We need to coordinate with state law enforcement from here to California. Start with the state police. We can't have her out there feeling all safe, thinking she's gotten away with it. In the meantime, Dr. Spencer is going to try and figure out exactly who we do have at the morgue."

"Do you want me to call a press conference?"

"I got that. We need to let the media in on this. I think you and Michael should get some uniformed officers and start canvassing the motel's neighborhood. Concentrate within a mile radius. Show her picture, ask some questions."

"Sure, I guess it's safe to say you're back on the case. You

want the lead back?"

"Is that okay with you?" She didn't want to step on his toes.

"Yeah, that's fine. My mind's all over the place, so it's probably better that you do. You know I've got your back. We've always been one hell of a team."

"Problem is, so was Mendoza and Henderson," Shevaughn admitted.

Since seeing the tape, something had been nagging him and he finally brought it up. Actually, it surprised him that neither one of them had thought of it before.

"It hasn't even crossed your mind, has it?"

"What?"

"Henderson and Mendoza, everyone's calling them the Fingertip Killers, but since all your biggest cases relate to cards, you do know what this one should be called?"

"I'm afraid you're gonna tell me."

"Deuces Wild."

Chapter Twenty-Six

DOLL CROSSED THE Arizona border by late Saturday afternoon. During her road trip, she disposed of Jamie's fingertips by throwing them out of the car window, one by one, as she traveled west. They were small enough not to attract attention. *Hopefully, they're buzzard food by now.*

She sat at a bar slowly nursing a drink, twirling the straw in her screwdriver as she looked around. One Eyed Jacks Sports Lounge in Show Low, Arizona actually sat over a Days Inn motel. Pretty convenient, too, since she refused to spend another night sleeping in that hot-ass car. It had been a bad day. When she woke up, it felt like100 degrees inside the car and she panicked. At first, she thought she was on fire. Then, when she tried to pay for breakfast, the restaurant rejected Jamie's credit card and she had to use her last few dollars. Talk about a rock and a hard place. She needed someone to take her home or at the least pay for a room downstairs.

The bar made her, a city girl, feel a little out of place. Its golden knotty pine, country western décor was country to the max. Then the door opened and in walked a tall, aristocratic-looking man with skin the color of butterscotch. The constant chatter in the lounge stopped and everyone watched his smooth stride. He went to the bar and sat next to the cute little lady all the cowboys had their eyes on. You

could feel the hostility in the room.

"It appears you could use some company. Mind if I join you?" He sat down before she answered and extended his hand. "I'm Malcolm Haulm. My friends call me Mal." He spoke with a slight southern twang. You could actually hear the years of education in his voice.

"Jamie Price," Doll lied, remembering the name on the rejected credit card.

"Nice meeting you, *Jamie*. Mind if I say that you don't look quite at home here?"

"Well, neither do you." They both chuckled in acknowledgement.

"Then I suggest that we go someplace where we feel more at home."

Doll reached for her drink.

"Leave it, my sweet," he said, taking her hand. "I think I have something more to your liking."

You certainly do, she thought, looking at his lips. They were actually prettier than hers! She also liked the hint of gray in his hairline. This would be the first time she would enjoy the company of such a distinguished-looking man.

As they walked to the exit, several men with pool cues gravitated towards the door effectively blocking the couple's exit.

"Gentlemen, I highly recommend you think twice before you try anything. I wouldn't want to ruin your night. The lady's with me." He brushed back the front of his jacket and flashed a glimpse of the pistol stuck in his waistband. The men slowly parted to let them pass.

She followed him outside to the parking lot and was impressed when he walked over to his brand new jet black Lincoln Continental. *It looks like Mr. Haulm has a lot of money and a lot of style.* He opened the door and she sunk into the luxurious tan leather interior. She reacted to the new car smell like an aphrodisiac.

"Where are we going?"

"Don't worry about it. I want to surprise you. Just sit back, relax and enjoy the ride."

He spent the next two hours driving to Tucson, yet to her it went by in a flash. Malcolm pulled up in front of the ℳ hotel. It was the most luxurious place she'd ever seen, let alone been in. She noticed everyone snapped to attention as soon as he stepped out of the car; from the valet to the doorman to the woman behind the reservation desk.

"Is my penthouse ready?" he asked, placing his briefcase on the counter.

"No sir, we are still renovating the penthouse, but the presidential suite is available, Mr. Haulm."

"That will do for tonight." He handed the briefcase to the attendant. Make sure it gets to my suite."

Wow, the presidential suite! A girl sure could get used to this.

They walked from the reservation desk to the bar and he ordered champagne.

"My apologies, Jamie. They weren't expecting me. It'll take a moment for them to make sure everything is up to par. In the meantime, I thought we could get better acquainted."

Doll gave him her rehearsed story about being tired of

living in a small town and how she had just hopped in her car and decided to go west. She wanted him to think of her as impulsive.

A man elegantly dressed in a tuxedo came up to Malcolm and whispered something into his ear. Malcolm stood up, took Doll's hand to help her off the bar stool and together they walked to a private elevator. She watched him insert the card key into the elevator's control panel. As they rode up to the eighteenth floor, Doll shyly slipped her hand back into his.

When Malcolm opened the doors to the suite, the sight was so overwhelming that she didn't know what to say. The three thousand square-foot suite was larger than any home she'd been in. In fact, she'd never seen a room this size outside of the day room in Juvie.

That's where the comparison ended. She walked around the beautifully decorated room that was outfitted in hues of brown, amber and gold while touching the various aspects of the plush accommodations. A fire burned in the stunning, stand-alone glass fireplace. The way the fireplace was designed gave one the impression that the fire was floating in mid-air. When Doll walked out onto the private terrace, she found an ice bucket filled with a bottle of 1979 Krug Clos de Mesnil champagne and two crystal flutes waiting for them. The view of the Catalina Mountains was breathtaking.

"Why don't you go get comfortable? I imagine you'd like to freshen up after all those hours on the road. You'll find there's a hot bath waiting for you. If you'd like, I'll bring you some champagne while you're relaxing in the tub."

Doll went into the bedroom and flopped down on the massive, king-size modern poster bed. Lying on her back,

she moved her arms up and down like a kid making snow angels. Everything smelled so clean.

Doll undressed and walked naked into the bathroom. The water in the Jacuzzi tub filled the room with the calming scent of lavender. As she sank into the warm, soothing water, a moan of satisfaction escaped her lips. *This must be what heaven feels like.* She ran the hot water until it covered her shoulders, wrung out the wash cloth and placed it on her forehead, closed her eyes and for the first time in days, she relaxed.

She heard the bathroom door open and continued to lie still with her eyes closed, waiting for him to come to her. The clink of the champagne glass against the tub and his body's proximity made her think he might try to kiss her. Instead, he left the flute, went to the shower, undressed and got in. When she heard the water running, Doll opened her eyes. She could see the outline of his golden body through the glass block shower wall. She finished the champagne in a couple of gulps, stepped out of the tub and walked to the shower stall soaking wet. When she opened the door, he pulled her in with him, kissing her face and neck. For a man of his age, he was in great shape and she enjoyed giving in. She wanted this to last as long as possible.

Jamie sure knows how to touch a man and get his mojo workin'. They left the shower and he picked her up, carried her to the bed and took her with an urgency he hadn't felt for a long time. By the time they left the bedroom, both had worked up quite an appetite. Malcolm called room service from the phone in the hotel's living room and ordered a crab-stuffed jumbo prawn appetizer to share, followed

by a salad consisting of romaine hearts, feta cheese and candied cashews with a strawberry-champagne vinaigrette. For the entrée, he asked for a double-cut porterhouse for two, garlic parmesan mashed potatoes and asparagus. He thought for a moment and added a bottle of Hennessey to his order. Putting his hand over the bottom of the receiver, he asked, "Would you care for dessert?" She shook her head "no" and he placed his order for raspberry sorbet.

While they waited for their food, he got his briefcase and took several prescription bottles out.

"Help yourself," he said and popped a couple. Doll picked a pretty blue and red capsule and washed it down with champagne.

Everything impressed her. When dinner arrived under silver-domed covers topped with knobs that looked like spades, it looked like a meal fit for royalty. He waited on her hand and foot. She had every intention of properly thanking him the only way she knew how, but the combination of the Amoxapine and alcohol ended the evening for her after the second snifter of Hennessey.

She awoke the next morning, naked between the wonderful 700-thread count, 100% Egyptian cotton Pratesi sheets. She rolled over to wake him, but he had gotten up before her. Doll put on the peach-colored silk spa robe and ventured into the living room. Thirsty, she spotted the Krug bottle, picked it up and drained the last corner of flat champagne. She went to get the remote off of the TV and under it she found a Haulm Industries business card lying on a stack of bills. On the back of the card, he'd scribbled a short note, "*Jamie, it's been real. If you're ever in Austin, look me up. Mal.*" Doll counted the money. A thousand dollars! She saw Texas in her future and her future looked a whole

lot brighter now.

She called down to the front desk to inquire about checking out. They informed her that Mr. Haulm instructed them she had to vacate by Monday afternoon, but she was welcome to use any and all of the hotel's amenities until then. Doll called room service to order breakfast, had the laundry pick up all her clothes and then she made an afternoon appointment with the masseuse at the hotel spa. She added a facial, manicure and pedicure to her session. When her Belgian waffle and sausage arrived, she turned on the TV and began to enjoy her breakfast in bed.

She switched to the news to see if there was any mention of her or Reuben. When nothing came up, she relaxed and enjoyed the rest of her stay. On her way to the spa, she went into the hotel boutique, bought a rather expensive bikini and put it on his tab. This was abso-fuckin'-lutely, the way she wanted to live.

It all ended way too soon. Eleven o'clock that night, as she watched TV in the hotel bed for the last time, CBS Sunday Night News broke the story.

"The search continues for Dahlia McMillan Henderson. Henderson, recently released from Juvenile Hall for the murder of her stepfather, is now the prime suspect in the deaths of at least six people. The police have come to the conclusion that the murders may have stopped since Mendoza, the apparent dominant mastermind of the pair, was fatally shot in Green Acres Mall early last week. Authorities have yet to apprehend Henderson, his alleged accomplice and they suspect she may be heading west. Authorities ask that folks in Arizona, California, New Mexico and Nevada to be especially observant. If you have any information regarding the whereabouts of Dahlia

McMillan Henderson, please call 1- (800) 567-TIPS.

"An added twist to the story...It seems that Lark McMillan, the mother of Dahlia Henderson and a victim of the duo, kept secret bank accounts dating back to 1966 where she compiled a small fortune. The police discovered it today while going through the victim's background and finances. A total of seventy-five thousand dollars has been found so far. The irony is that, as the only living relative, Ms. Henderson would have inherited the money, except now she's implicated in her mother's murder."

When they mentioned Arizona, Doll got a chill. *How the hell did they come up with that? Now they were too close for comfort.* At first, she felt relief when she heard that the police thought Reuben ran things. Then she got angry. *They don't think I have the brains to pull off what we did?*

And where the hell did Mom get seventy-five thousand dollars? She should have told me. It might have kept her alive a little longer. She looked around the room at what real money could buy. Doll didn't know how she was gonna get her hands on it, but now Texas would have to wait.

Doll wasn't the only one who watched the Sunday Night News. Several patrons from One Eyed Jacks remembered the little lady leaving the bar with that guy. Most of them were happy to dial the 1-800 number and report seeing the suspect accompanied by a Black man with a gun.

Chapter Twenty-Seven

WHEN DOLL RELUCTANTLY left the luxurious ℳ
hotel, she worried about how she would get back to One
Eyed Jacks for Jamie's car. She asked the concierge to call
her a taxi and he told her that wouldn't be necessary since
her car was already waiting for her. When the valet pulled
up in the shiny, black Lincoln Continental, she thought the
concierge and valet were fucking with her head. They
assured her that the car now belonged to her, compliments
of Mr. Haulm. She noticed he'd even had the car detailed
inside and out and the gas tank was full. This was quite the
souvenir for the best weekend she'd ever spent. Happily,
she got on the road and headed east, back to New York.
She only stopped to rest during the night. Both nights she
stayed in a motel along the interstate and each night she
compared her subpar accommodations to the lush hotel.
She used the three-day drive to try to come up with a way
to get her hands on her money, but nothing materialized. It
made her sick to her stomach when she remembered that
she didn't even have her I.D. anymore. *This is fucked up.*
Everything, except her meeting Malcolm, had gone
downhill since she listened to Reuben.

She couldn't make up her mind about her next move
and things got worse when she crossed the New Mexico
border and drove across the tip of Texas, past Amarillo.

Something in the back of her mind kept telling her to detour to Austin. After all, as an experienced and obviously intelligent businessman, maybe Malcolm could help her get to her money. Then again, if he'd seen the news bulletin, he knew the police wanted her for murder. Unwilling to take the chance, Doll stayed on Route 66 until she left Texas and entered Oklahoma.

"The phones haven't stopped ringing since last night," Jared informed Shevaughn as soon as she stepped into their office. "Most of the calls were from Show Low, Arizona. I don't know why, but she must have thought it was safe for her to come out of hiding or maybe there was a reason she had to."

"She thinks she's gotten away by exchanging identities. Why would she be afraid to be seen? Did any of the callers give you a description?"

"Yeah, sounds like she made some changes to her appearance. I already sent the descriptions and the most current picture we could find to a sketch artist. We should be getting a new sketch any minute now."

"Good. What did you do, spend the night here?"

"I couldn't find a reason to go home."

"How is Kennedy?"

"She must have told her family about Lori and Jared Junior. I'm off her hospital visitor's list."

"Well, maybe once you get her home you can work it out. I know she loves you, Jared. Right now, she's hurt and rightfully so."

"I guess that could happen...if she ever comes home.

Between the therapy and constant care she'll need, that's starting to look like a long shot. I wouldn't put any money on it."

"Have faith, little brother. Honestly, what else can you do?"

Jamie's dad was frantic. Since he'd lost his wife to breast cancer in 1981, he and his daughter made a point of meeting for Sunday dinner at least once a month. Sometimes they would cook for each other and other times they'd meet at a restaurant. Last Wednesday, she suggested they go all out and celebrate his birthday by meeting at Cipriani's in Manhattan. She knew he had a fascination with the Mafia and that made it even more special. Sunday, he put on his best suit and drove to the city. When his daughter never showed up, he'd gone to her apartment and then to the drugstore. Her boss said he had to call someone in to take her shifts because he hadn't seen or heard from her since Wednesday. *Where the hell was she?* No one knew.

When he called the Portsborough Police to report Jamie missing, they asked him to come in to fill out a missing persons' report and to bring a recent photo with him. As soon as the officer saw the picture, he noticed the resemblance to the revised picture of Dahlia from the new sketch on the flyer. He took Mr. Price's completed report and sent it with a copy of the photo to Homicide. As soon as Shevaughn saw the picture, she knew. *It's not a coincidence.*

"Jared, I want a list of all Jamie Price's credit card transactions since Wednesday morning. Michael, take this new sketch and a couple of officers and show it to anyone

within a mile's radius of the Rexall drugstore where Ms. Price worked. I'm going to go to her apartment and see if I can find anything that will point us in the right direction. I'm afraid this has gone from a missing person's case to a homicide."

Shevaughn hadn't known that Mr. Price stood on the other side of her door when she made that statement. They heard a pained roar and then a thud. Jared and Michael rushed to the source of the sound and found Mr. Price on his knees, leaning against the wall. He looked at the two men and got a glimpse of Shevaughn standing behind them. He directed his question to her.

"Jamie's dead? Murdered?"

"Sir, I'm so sorry. We have to wait for confirmation from the coroner."

"Where is she? I need to go to her."

"Sir, we can't be sure until the coroner finishes the examination.

"I...I have to make arrangements. When can I have her?"

"Once she's identified. It's the coroner's top priority. Call and leave the information with Detective Walker after you've chosen a funeral home. When and if she's identified, we'll take care of the transfer arrangements."

All the wind had been knocked out of Mr. Price's sails. The man had no energy to argue.

"Yes, I'll call you with the details."

The phone rang as Detective Walker escorted Mr. Price out.

"Detective Benjamin, Homicide."

"I need you and Von to come to the coroner's office so I can explain the results of the toxicology screening."

"We're on our way."

Dr. Spencer was waiting for them, pacing when they arrived. He didn't even say good morning.

"Okay, so first things first. We have positively indentified Ms. Price. The toxicology report estimates the woman had almost 900 milligrams of Methaqualone in her system. That's Quaaludes in street talk. Most likely, that amount would have at least rendered her unconscious before the attack, thus no defensive wounds. There were exactly twelve stab wounds and just as many blows to the head. This all happened after someone crushed her windpipe. We have another case of extreme overkill.

"I did get a miniscule amount of saliva from her labia which would suggest sexual contact. However, I found no evidence of penetration which substantiates, along with the hormone levels in the saliva, that the perpetrator was a woman."

"And you narrowed down the time of death?" Shevaughn hoped that would answer her next question.

"Because the thermostat had been turned up, that got a little tricky. The best I can do is an educated guess. Based on her stomach contents, I'd say she died Wednesday night between seven p.m. and midnight. I'm leaning towards earlier rather than later."

"So it's possible she wasn't the one using her debit card for gas at eleven Wednesday night."

"I'd say very possible."

"So, it looks like Jamie Price died simply because of her resemblance. Dahlia only killed her to throw us off track. And it *almost* worked!" Shevaughn surmised.

But almost doesn't count. Instead, it added victim six to the tally.

Chapter Twenty-Eight

THURSDAY MORNING'S WEATHER was so beautiful Doll forgot about her worries. She woke up early in her motel room, showered, dressed and quickly ate a breakfast of two donuts and coffee at the nearby diner. Doll was ready to get back on the road. She wanted her money.

The sky was a cloudless blue and Doll, anxious and excited, enjoyed the last leg of her journey home, so much so that she didn't even think about it when traffic slowed down until she saw the reason why. A small roadblock stood in the way of all her plans.

She'd pushed the problem of how she would get her hands on the money her mother left to her to the back of her mind. Things always had a way of working out the way she wanted them to, didn't they? Yet suddenly here she sat, staring at her obstacle. She looked behind her just in time to see another car pull in close, blocking her retreat. They had her trapped. She thought about the gun Reuben took from her before going to the mall to die. *Poor, stupid bastard.* At that moment, she wished she hadn't focused so much on getting her mother's money and she definitely regretted not heading for Texas instead of New York.

It was difficult to assess the situation without panicking. She saw no way to leave the road without attracting the

policemen's attention. Her only hope was to try to speed past the police car that blocked the road. And if a cop got in her way, oh well. Doll broke out in a sweat as the car inched closer to the roadblock. When she got to the front of the line, she sat and waited until the policeman walked toward her. As he approached her driver's side window, Doll gunned the engine. The car lurched forward, dangerously brushing past the officer, causing him to jump out of the way. She clipped the left fender of the police car and for one sweet second, she thought she was home free.

Suddenly, a second police car sped from the far left side of the road, crossed the center of the road and turned into her lane. To avoid him, she made a sharp right, causing her to run into a ditch. She pressed the accelerator and tried to go in reverse to get away from the police car descending on her, but all she heard was the sound of the tires of her own car spinning their way into mud. Doll jumped out of the car and tried to run across the field next to the road. Two officers left their cars and were in hot pursuit. After running as fast as she could for almost five minutes, she definitely felt the effects of all her smoking and drinking. Doll dropped to her knees, coughing and choking. She couldn't go on.

Shevaughn hung up the phone and sat down. She found it hard to believe. It was finally over.

"They've got her," she announced to Jared and Michael.

"What? When?"

"Just now. She tried to get through the road block set up on Route 17. They're bringing her here since the first murder happened in our jurisdiction. We're going with a

couple of officers to the Tappan Zee Bridge entrance to make the custody transfer."

Although Shevaughn had an idea of what Dahlia Henderson looked like, when they arrived at the Tappan Zee, no one was prepared for the irony of seeing the diminutive-looking girl sitting in the back seat of the patrol car. With an angelic face, she couldn't have been a hundred pounds soaking wet and she surely didn't look capable of murder – especially the gruesome murders she committed. Something about her facade made you want to protect her. Shevaughn understood why her mother nicknamed her Doll.

When she noticed the car up on the bed of the tow truck, her first thought was *how can she afford that car?* Then she realized it was the car from her drowning dream! *Coincidence? Or had Ariel been trying to warn her way back then? Her determination to work on this case had certainly caused her marriage to sink.* She snapped out of her deep thoughts and returned to the present.

The officers that arrived with Shevaughn transferred the tiny young woman, restrained in tie wraps, to their patrol car. The standard handcuffs and shackles that the state police used were too large for Doll's wrists. The Feds informed Shevaughn that although Ms. Henderson was now under Portsborough's jurisdiction, there would be pending state and federal criminal charges and she would probably be facing the death penalty. No one spoke on the ride back to the precinct.

When they got back, Shevaughn and Jared put Dahlia in a small, soundproof, interrogation room with three chairs and a desk. One chair and the desk were bolted to the floor. Three of the walls were bare and the fourth was mirrored.

Jared used another tie wrap to restrain one of Doll's wrists to the chair and he sat behind the desk. Shevaughn pulled the other chair in front of Dahlia and sat peering into her face. Jared read Doll her rights, "You have the right to remain silent. Anything you say can and will be used against you in a court of law. You have the right to speak to an attorney. If you cannot afford an attorney, one will be appointed to you. Do you understand each of these rights I have explained to you?" Shevaughn added, "Having these rights in mind, do you wish to talk to us now?"

"Sure, why not? You probably already know most of it anyway."

"But before we start, I have to ask. Who killed your stepfather?"

Shevaughn saw the surprise cross Doll's face. Instantly, it vanished.

"Oh, come on, that's old news."

"No, I want to hear your version."

"Look, either charge me or let me go."

"Sure, have it your way. You are being charged with six counts of first degree murder in connection with the deaths of: Dominic Brazza, Wilbur Moss, two unidentified victims…"

"That would be Grady Evans and LaShawn…Well, I never did get her last name," Doll stated without any sign of emotion.

"…your mother, Lark McMillan…"

When she got to Mrs. McMillan, Shevaughn's voice cracked. *The woman had been genuinely concerned and suspicious of her daughter. For her to turn around and burn her*

own mother alive...

"Kinda like your own version of personally sending her to Hell." Shevaughn said in a hushed tone.

"What? What did you say?"

"I said it's like you were punishing her. Why? Did she kill him? It was her, wasn't it? Not you."

"That's a dead issue, pun intended. You weren't finished with the victim list. "

...and Jamie Price," Shevaughn said without skipping a beat.

Doll was visibly shaken by the unexpected twist, but she continued with her façade of bravado. Only the slight rattle of the shackles made her tremor apparent.

"Yeah, yeah, they're gone and I'm not. What do you want? I did it...I mean, I helped Reuben pull it off, but if I hadn't he would have killed me too. You saw what he was capable of. He scared me, but I still loved him. I wish I could tell you why. If I don't understand, how could you?"

"What wouldn't I understand? The powerful feeling you got from forbidden sex, especially when you knew that someone would die in the process? It added to the rush, didn't it? I bet you got to the point where the simple act of making love didn't do it for you anymore...it probably bored the hell out of you. After all, you've been seducing men all your life. This took it to a whole new level, didn't it? Tell me, after the first time, after Mr. Brazza, did you start to crave the bloodlust the same way you craved the alcohol and drugs? Did you need it?"

As she asked the questions, Shevaughn slapped graphic photos of the victims down on the table. It made her cringe

when she caught a slight smirk and the look of satisfaction on Doll's face.

Doll tilted her head and scrutinized Shevaughn with a puzzled glance. She had a hint of surprise and new appreciation in her eyes. *Maybe she did have a clue!* She looked straight at the detective and smiled, just a little.

"I suppose you got that out of some psych manual. Don't pretend you know me. We just wanted to get even."

"I asked you a question. That implies I don't understand, but I'm trying to. I just can't wrap my head around the fingertip thing or why you killed your mother?"

Doll suddenly burst into tears.

"I know she tried to blame it all on me. But it was him. You wanna know why? Reuben said they longer it took to identify the bodies, the longer we'll be free. I did it 'cause he wanted me to. There was nothing I wouldn't do for him. I thought he felt the same." *He definitely did.*

"Are you sure that's how it went down? It's funny because you removed Wilbur's fingertips, yet left him at his home. He was the only one victim you had a history with and you didn't hide his identity?

"I get the distinct feeling the opposite is true. He was your puppet. I think he worshiped you and you knew it. You took advantage and used him. He tried to do the right thing; he found a place for the two of you to live, a job to help take care of you. And at the end, right before he died, I saw the regret in his eyes and so far I've seen none from you. Why is that?"

Doll realized the detective made sense. That's when

everything had started going wrong. It had nothing to do with Reuben, Wilbur's identity had led to their downfall. She wished she'd kept her word and found them the PYT she had promised. However, she would never admit it aloud, so she answered Shevaughn's last question.

"Because regret would imply that I'm guilty...and I'm not. I think it's time I asked for a lawyer."

"We'll see about getting you a court-appointed attorney."

"No, I want a real attorney, not some overworked slob who doesn't have a clue."

"Can you afford an attorney?"

"I could if I use the money Mom left me."

"There is no money, Ms. Henderson."

A look of disbelief crossed Doll's face.

"But...on the news...it said..."

"What I told them to say. I thought that might get your attention."

Doll jumped up and tried to reach for Shevaughn, but the bolted chair and the tie wrap held her back.

"So, bitch, you're telling me there is no money? You lied?"

"Honey, I would do whatever it took to get you here."

"I'm not saying another word."

"Suit yourself. Collectively, we have enough evidence to put you away for a long time. Jared, can you see that she's booked and put in a holding cell until her attorney arrives? Good luck, Ms. Henderson." Shevaughn sashayed out of

the room.

♣♣♣

Finishing up the Henderson report, Shevaughn left the precinct and headed home feeling rather pleased with how everything turned out. Ariel's advice had worked like a charm and helped her close the case.

When she unlocked her front door, her home smelled like Little Italy. Nonna and Toni were in the kitchen starting dinner, so she went to see what her little man was up to. She watched as DJ cooed and tried to reach for the mobile hanging over his crib. Shevaughn scooped him up and blew kisses on his neck. He let out a hearty chuckle and she laughed along with him until the doorbell rang.

Carrying him like a football, she went to the door. When she opened it, a young man in a tan leisure suit handed her an envelope.

"Mrs. Williams? You've been served." He turned and left before she had time to react. *What the hell?* She opened the envelope and saw that Marcus was suing her for full custody of the kids, not just his son, but Toni, too! *Son-of-a-bitch could've told me first.* She went to the phone and dialed The Nook.

"Marc, I just got your papers and if you think you can take my kids without a fight, you're highly mistaken."

"I won't discuss this with you on the phone, Von. You need to talk to your lawyer. Have him call mine." Before she could answer, he hung up.

Shevaughn heard the dial tone and was livid. She grabbed the Yellow Pages from the bookshelf in the office to look for a divorce attorney that specialized in child

custody. After perusing through the options, she reconsidered phoning a lawyer immediately and called Mattie instead.

"Hey girl, you ain't gonna believe this. Marc is trying to get full custody of both kids."

"What? You need a good lawyer."

"I know. That's why I'm calling you. Got any recommendations?"

"I do taxes for a couple of divorce attorneys. Let me get you their numbers. I'll call you right back."

"Okay, thanks."

She couldn't bear to just sit there and wait, so she grabbed an empty box from the storage closet and went to their bedroom with the intent of packing up the remainder of his things. The kids were the only reminder of him she wanted left in her house.

Shevaughn went into their bathroom, but he'd taken all his colognes, razors, shaving cream and personal items with him when he left. She returned to the bedroom, sat down on the bed and looked at the tall Alder bookcase's top two shelves. They contained all his books. He was fascinated with history, which bored Shevaughn because she read for the sheer pleasure of it. Sometimes a good novel helped her forget about reality and that helped in her line of work.

She got the stepladder from the kitchen, brought it back to the bedroom, opened it until the latch caught and stood up on it. Shevaughn pulled the books from the shelf and tossed them to the bed to save trips. One bounced open and she spotted the corner of a newspaper article peeking

from behind the cover. She got down from the stool and was struck by a feeling of dread as she picked it up. Her feeling was confirmed when she discovered that she was holding a newspaper article about the Roland Johnson case, back in '85. She then held each book by its front and back covers and began shaking them over the bed before putting them in the box. Out fell more clippings and all of them were about her. Some of them went as far back as 1981. *These belong to Marcus!* He had been following her career from the very beginning. *Wait, so he knew about me before we met?* She thought back to the first time they'd spoken. *Had he made that heartless comment on purpose?* Suddenly, she got the distinct feeling that she'd been played. *What the hell is going on?*

The phone rang. Mattie had the names of two lawyers. She jotted them down and then decided to confide in her friend.

"Can I ask you something?"

"Sure, you know you can ask me anything. What's up?"

"When I met Marc, he gave me the impression that he didn't know anything about me until after we talked. That's when he supposedly did a little investigating and found out what I did for living. What if I told you I just found some newspaper clippings about me from years before we met and they aren't mine? That would mean he's a liar, wouldn't it?"

"Sounds like that to me. You're sure they aren't yours? Maybe you saved them and forgot about it?"

"If they were I wouldn't have stuck them in the pages of his history books."

"No argument there."

"Besides, I had to use the stepladder to get to the books, so I think I'd remember if I went through the trouble of storing them like that." She stopped and counted the clippings.

"There are seventeen clippings spanning a total of eight years. Mattie, that's my entire career! We've only been married for three."

"Girl, I think getting him out of your life may be the best thing that's happened to you."

"You know I'm going to have to talk to him."

"Maybe you should leave it alone. He doesn't know that you know."

"Now you know that ain't me. I'm gonna get to the bottom of this."

"Well, be careful and good luck. Call me after you talk to him, okay?"

"Will do. Wish me luck."

"If this turns out like I think, you'll need it."

Hanging up, Shevaughn immediately called Marcus.

"Book Nook, Marcus speaking."

"We need to talk," she stated without saying hello.

"If this is about the custody suit, I told you to speak with my lawyer."

"No Marc, this is about us, just you and me."

"We have nothing to talk about. It's over, or don't you get that?" She heard the anger in his voice. *Good, now we're both mad.*

"Oh, I get it, but I have some unanswered questions and

need a little clarification. I don't want to do it over the phone. How 'bout we meet, say, in an hour at the Olive Garden on 10th and Commonwealth?"

"Somewhere nice and public so you have plenty of witnesses, huh? You're not afraid to be alone with me, are you?"

She dismissed his question as if it were ridiculous.

"Yeah, right," she answered in a sarcastic tone. "I just think it's better for both of us. See you in a little while." She hung up before he had time to reconsider.

Shevaughn collected the clippings and changed clothes, purposely wearing the same outfit she'd worn in Atlantic City the day Marcus proposed to her. She hadn't quite dropped all the baby fat and it fit a little tighter now, but she hoped it would bring back memories of what he'd lost. She touched up her makeup, gave DJ to Nonna and told her she'd be back in a bit. As she walked around to the rear of her car, she dropped the box of books into the trunk and headed for the restaurant.

Marcus arrived at the restaurant ten minutes early, got a table and ordered a glass of their house red to help calm his nerves. During the drive over, he'd tried to figure out what she wanted to talk about, but he told himself it didn't matter as long as she wanted to see him. As angry as he seemed about their current state of affairs, he missed married life and being with Kennedy in her condition sure didn't help the mood around Mom and Pop's house.

The doctors were amazed that his sister's condition was slowly improving. They said it was because she attacked physical therapy with the same effort she attacked

everything in life, giving 110 percent. He thought she did it to show Jared she could get on with her life, but many a night he heard her softly crying herself to sleep. No one in that house was very happy at the present moment.

He watched the waitress lead Shevaughn to him and involuntarily licked his lips. She was wearing the Atlantic City outfit she'd worn the night he proposed. He thought that was a good sign. However, her first words dashed his hopes.

"You left your books, so I decided to pack them up for you and you'll never guess what I found." She reached into her purse, pulled out the newspaper clippings neatly held together with a paperclip and slammed them on the table.

Shit. He could kick his own ass for forgetting about them. He hadn't added any new ones to his collection since their wedding day.

"Von, I can explain."

"I bet you can, but these indicate that you knew all about me long before we met. So...you put on this little charade and lied to me from the very beginning? Why?"

"Okay, yes, I did know about you before we met. What's the big deal?"

"What's the big deal? You lied and pretended you didn't know me. You acted like you didn't know what calling me 'heartless' would do when you knew all along it would push my buttons. You used it to unsettle me and I have to say it worked. Your little apology was just as bogus. You knew exactly what you were apologizing for. Everything we had is built on a lie, so I guess we didn't have much, did we?"

"Look, Von, I was wrong. I admit it. I should have told you I've been following your career for while. You fascinated me. You seemed to be a woman who had it all together. I just wanted to meet you. I didn't know I'd fall in love with you."

"I bet all his time you've been patting yourself on the back. You really suckered me and reeled me in, didn't you? I wonder what the courts will say when they find out what a lying manipulator you are. That's not the best example of someone you'd want raising children."

"Everything wasn't a lie and one has nothing to do with the other."

"We'll see if the judge feels the same." Shevaughn got up from the table and faced him. "You don't get it, do you? If I can't trust you, I damn sure can't live with you. Come get your damn books or I'm leaving them on the sidewalk."

She quickly turned and walked out of the Olive Garden. Marcus threw a five dollar bill on the table and hastily followed, just in time to see the box thrown from the trunk of her car. Books scattered everywhere. She hurried to the driver's door and pulled off as he ran to gather them. Shevaughn sped away without looking back.

Chapter Twenty-Nine

DOLL PACED UP and down within her 8-foot by 6-foot cell after her third meeting with her state-appointed attorney. Donald Symonds looked too old to be up-to-date when it came to the latest laws. Sitting across the table from him, she tested him by making a sexual suggestion while touching his knee. He hastily brushed her hand aside as if he found her touch repugnant. She bristled at the thought that she'd actually met a man who refused her advances. He didn't seem to find her attractive. It made a small dent in her confidence. She hated feeling powerless over him or the situation. Besides, she didn't want a lawyer she couldn't manipulate. At this rate, she would be looking at a very long jail sentence. He proposed that she plead guilty and throw herself on the mercy of the court. In essence, he wanted her to beg for her life. Well, she didn't feel like begging and besides, she wasn't good at it. She needed someone to help her find a competent attorney.

When a probably once attractive, now beer-bellied guard walked passed her cell, she put her face against the bars and slowly licked her lips, touching the tip of her nose with her tongue. She watched as he stood in front of her to block anyone from seeing her little show. Now that she had his full attention, she lay spread-eagled on the cot. She knew the troll wanted her when he looked up and down

the hall to make sure no one could see what they were doing. She sucked her index finger and began to masturbate in front of him. She knew she had him when she saw his erection. Doll got up, walked towards him, reached between the bars and stroked his crotch. It had been a while since she seduced a man and even though she found him disgusting, giving him an expert hand job excited her.

"Can you imagine what I could do if these bars weren't between us?" she whispered as he came in her hand. "Figure something out and get back to me."

The next day he came to her cell and escorted her down to the showers. She eagerly made good on her promise. This went on for several days as she taught him some new tricks and relived old ones. Doll allowed him every liberty except intercourse. By the time she got around to asking him if he could help her find a good lawyer, he couldn't help but say yes. When he agreed, she made him lay down and she got on top, finally allowing him to penetrate her. She gave him the ride of his life.

The following Monday afternoon, Doll sat in the visiting area and waited. Her horny guard appeared with an attractive, caramel man in tow. *He couldn't be more than a few years older than me!* She liked what she saw. *This could turn out all right!*

"Hello, Ms. Henderson. I'm Sharrod Campbell, your new attorney."

♣♣♣

Jared sat in his car, watching the Williams home for quite some time before he got up enough nerve to ring the bell and demand to see his wife. *Screw this, all they can say*

is no. He got out of the car and walked up to the porch with a determined stride. His stomach churned when he pressed the doorbell and while he waited for someone to answer, he willed it to settle down.

When his father-in-law answered the door, he found himself at a loss for words.

"What are you doing here?"

"Sir, I've come to get my wife and bring her home. I thought, maybe with enough time, she'd realize that she needs me. But how can she when you all are waiting on her hand and foot? I know we have problems, but I made this mistake. No, what I mean is, the act may have been a mistake, but my son isn't. You should understand. As a man, I have to do my best to be a good father to him. This all happened way before we were a couple, hell, even before Von and Marcus were a couple. I love your daughter and hiding from our problems won't make them go away. She needs to be with me so I can take care of her. I meant it when I vowed for better or worse, in sickness and in health. Now, sir, can I *please* speak with my wife?"

He felt a glimmer of hope when Darien said nothing and stepped out of his way.

She parked the *fuckin' chair* in front of her window seat. The words were always connected in her mind, although she never said them aloud. Kennedy sat in her *fuckin' chair*, looking out the window, all the while missing being able to sit in her window seat and lean her face against the cold glass. It had been one of her favorite spots while growing up in her childhood home. Things she'd taken for granted all her life were still there, just out of her reach. When you

can walk, you can't imagine what losing that ability will do to you when you can't.

Her recovery was going well. She could now pull herself along on the parallel bars and, according to her therapist, it was a big accomplishment in such a short time. Kennedy noticed that it did improve her upper body strength. She needed that in order to get around in her fuckin' chair. She had only been out of the hospital a little over three weeks.

Her thoughts were interrupted as she watched Jared pull up in front of her house. For a while, she thought he would just sit there and not get out of the car. Then after about fifteen minutes, the car door opened and he did. She watched him walk up the sidewalk to her front door. *Had he lost weight?* Kennedy wondered if he would get past her father. When she heard the knock on her bedroom door, she knew he must have made a very convincing speech.

"Come in."

Although the embers of anger flamed, they were extinguished when he opened the door and she saw the distraught look on his handsome face. As he came closer, she confirmed his weight loss. She watched him hesitantly walk in. He'd always been pretty sure of himself, that was one of the things she loved about him, but now...

His eyes swept the room, taking in the hospital bed and her in the chair. He slowly walked over, knelt by her wheelchair and rested his head in her lap. She couldn't stop herself from stroking his cotton-soft, black hair. *God help me, I still love him.* And this wasn't just a sexual connection. It encompassed all the feelings attached to wanting to spend the rest of your life with that one special person. All they were missing was trust and respect. She wondered if

those virtues would ever return to their marriage. When he looked up at her, Kennedy knew she wanted to try.

"Babe, please don't be mad at me for coming. I had to see you. I don't know how long you intend to punish me, but I had to take the chance. I'd cut off my right arm if it would make things right. If you weren't so upset, maybe you would have paid more attention to driving and been able to avoid your accident, so I blame myself and I need to find a way to make everything up to you.

"When your Dad called from the hospital, I knew it happened right after you left her apartment. I wish I could take those moments back, change the outcome, but we both know that's impossible. Still, I believe our marriage is worth fighting for. Whether you admit it or not, we need each other and I'm not ashamed to say I miss not having you with me. The house is so quiet with you gone. Kennedy, please baby, come home with me and let me help you. Let me take you to your physical therapy sessions and work with you, not only to get you back, but to help you walk again. I swear we can make this work. Your health and our marriage are worth working hard for."

He could see her struggling to get her words together before she spoke.

"You know, Jared, between lying in my bed or sitting in this chair, I've had a lot of time to think about us…about everything. I remember the first time I laid eyes on you. I told Marcus I didn't think I could scare you. Now I realize you were afraid that by telling me the truth, you would lose me. I blamed and cursed you for everything that happened to me. Yeah, I was angry when you told me you wanted to wait to have kids, but you could have explained

it all then.

I don't know, maybe I could have handled it if you'd told me as soon as you knew you were a father, if you hadn't kept it a secret all these months. But that's beside the point because you didn't, you kept it from me. And that's a lie by omission. Then to add insult to injury, she named him after you. Do you know how much it hurt when I heard that? I wanted to kill all three of you. He was supposed to be *our* son. I felt like she stole everything from me.

"Then I realized how wrong I was to hate the boy. He didn't ask to be born under these circumstances and it wasn't as if you cheated on me, but keeping the truth from me turned out to be your biggest mistake," she felt her eyes burn as the tears started to form. *Damn it.* She didn't want to cry again, but looking at his face and feeling her loss gave her no choice.

"Look, I know hiding him from you was cowardly. I should have told you and we could have worked it out together, but you're right, I didn't want to lose you and I damn sure didn't want it to come to this. And just so you know, I'm coming totally clean. That's not the end of my problems. Now I think I'm under investigation on a morality charge. Someone dropped a dime on me, but if you and I can fix this, I can face whatever as long as we're together. I'd like us all to be family."

"Umh...as for dropping the dime...that would be me during my, I'm-gonna-make him-pay phase," Kennedy confessed. "You hurt me, so I hurt you back, plain and simple. Well, I thought it was, but I was sorry as soon as I hung up the phone.

"But if you're asking me if the four of us can live happily

ever after, you've lost your fuckin' mind. I don't see that happening. It's pretty damn obvious I have more important issues to deal with now and I think that's one too many."

"I thought the more support, the better. Lori said she's willing to come live with us and take care of you and baby." She noticed he didn't say his name.

"Well if she is, it means she's so in love with you that she's a bigger fool than I am. That also means that she would do anything to keep you. I'm not living under the same roof with that woman or your son, whether or not we were a couple when you two..." She still couldn't say it aloud and her voice trailed off.

"Mom, Dad and I have already discussed getting a nurse, that is, if I were to come home with you."

"So you were thinking about it?"

"I did the math. It had to happen before Mrs. Knight's funeral and that's the first time I noticed you. And yes, if I said I didn't miss you, I'd be lying. It's just gonna take me some time to forgive you. Now that I know about your son, I think you need to make arrangements to bring him to our house for visits instead of you going over there alone. And no, I won't go with you when you go see your son at her apartment. If she's willing to leave her home and move in with us, I don't think she'd object to you bringing him to our home, do you?"

"I'll arrange it. So you're really thinking about coming home?" She heard the tremor of joy and disbelief in his voice.

"You need to modify the house so it's wheelchair accessible. When you're finished making the changes, ask Dad to stop by and he will check it out. When it passes his

inspection, you can come get me."

"Is there anything else you need me to do to welcome you home?"

"Just don't look at me with pity in your eyes. If I see it, I'm gone. And don't rush me. Let me do this in my own time."

His heart jumped when she said the words "our home".

"You'll get all the time you need," Jared promised, knowing he'd do everything in his power to win her back. He thanked God that it was now a possibility.

"Would you mind putting me back in bed?"

Without a word he got off his knees, walked to her bed and turned down the covers. Coming back for her, Jared gently picked her up from her chair as if she were weightless. She wrapped her arms around his neck, placing her face next to his. He didn't realize he was crying until she softly touched his cheek to brush away his tears.

Chapter Thirty

READY FOR BATTLE, Shevaughn, Marcus and their respective attorneys appeared in court for their divorce and custody hearing. It didn't go the way either of them had anticipated. They didn't understand why the judge seemed so adamant about joint custody, especially once she learned that both of them had family willing and able to pitch in whenever necessary. After she heard about the newspaper articles, she stipulated that they attend counseling, both separate and as a couple for a minimum of six weeks before she'd even consider ruling on the divorce. The courtroom went silent as they both sat, stunned by her decision. Did someone karate-chop the fat lady in the neck and make her stop singing? Was this a chance to overcome the lack of trust between them so that they could salvage their marriage? Marcus hoped that they would while Shevaughn left the courthouse doubtful that they ever could.

It was Monday night, December eighteenth, exactly one week before Christmas, 1989. Even though New Years' Eve would probably mess with her head, Shevaughn felt grateful that the year was almost over. It wasn't only because of her personal trials and tribulations. It had been a hard year for a lot of folks. The one high point was the Berlin Wall coming down, symbolically ending the Cold

War. Other than that, everyone would probably remember it as the year the Exxon Valdez oil spill threatened the ecology or that Hurricane Hugo and the San Francisco earthquake killed over one hundred people. It was the year of disasters; some natural, some manmade. Her marriage qualified as the latter.

With the baby sleep, it almost felt like the good old BMW (before Marcus Williams) days. Nonna, Toni, Shevaughn and Kayla watched "I Love Lucy, the Christmas Special". It hadn't been on TV since 1956. This episode explained how Lucy told Ricky she was expecting. Without meaning to, Shevaughn remembered his reaction when she'd given Marcus the news. Everything had seemed so perfect then. The episode ended with an appearance by the 'real' Santa Claus on Christmas morning.

"There's no such thing as Santa Claus," eight-year old Toni announced at the end of the show.

"What?"

"I don't believe some fat guy comes to our house and gives us stuff. I can see him bringing *Honey, I Shrunk the Kids*, *Look Who's Talking* and Nigerian Barbie, but how's he gonna get my bike down the chimney without breaking it? And he'd never fit unless he went on a diet last summer!"

Nonna and Shevaughn laughed at her astute observation. Their little girl was growing up.

The phone rang and Shevaughn got up from the couch to answer it. On her way, she heard Toni tell Nonna, "Besides, even if there was one, the only way he could know is if Ariel told him. And I just told her about Nigerian Barbie last night." She hadn't realized Ariel still

talked to her daughter. Shevaughn mistakenly thought Ariel's visits ended when her marriage did.

When she answered and heard his voice, she resigned herself to being as cooperative as possible. After all, it was Christmas.

"Hello, Marcus. I suppose you're calling to finalize our Christmas visitation?"

"I wanted to ask if all of us could spend the day together and, if it's okay by you, maybe I could stay for Christmas dinner?"

Shevaughn hadn't anticipated his request, but she quickly decided not to fight it.

"Well...yeah, you could come over Christmas morning, watch Toni open her presents, stay for dinner and then you can take them to your apartment. I'll pick them up the following Saturday."

"I can keep them longer if you have plans."

Not very subtle, are you?

"No, I'll get them Saturday like I said. "

"That's fine. I'm closing The Nook between Christmas and..."

They both knew he was going to say New Year's, a holiday that now left a bitter taste in both their mouths.

Epilogue

ON HER BEST behavior, Doll refrained from making any sexual advances or innuendos while in the presence of Mr. Campbell, even though she wanted to. She liked how he got things done. First, he petitioned the court for a change of venue for the trial, stating that all the local publicity would prejudice jurors against her. Next, he saw that she got a makeover, accentuating her doll-like qualities. Dressed in a pink and white jumper with a crisp white blouse that tied at the neck, she looked so innocent folks thought of Mary Ingalls from Little House on the Prairie. Her hair was now back to its natural color and one of her inmates braided it for her court appearance. She looked nothing like a mass murderer and sexy would be the last thing on the jurors' minds when they saw her.

She sat at the defendant's table and watched as he eliminated the younger potential jurors. He told her that older people would have a hard time believing that such a little, pretty young thing could be capable of six wanton murders. He needed that to counteract the horribly graphic crime scene photos. Then they watched edited clips of the

tape and she could tell by the jurors' faces they weren't falling for her story of Reuben being the master manipulator behind it all and her role was that of the unwilling accomplice. When the coroner's report proved the police killed Reuben days before Jamie Price's death, it hammered the final nail in her coffin. If she had been capable of that murder, then it stood to reason that she committed the others. By the time they heard Jared and Shevaughn's testimony, the decision boiled down to guilty or not guilty by reason of insanity.

Although Doll fought against it, Mr. Campbell convinced her to take the insanity plea. It would be the only way she could avoid the death penalty. After several mental examinations by various psychiatric entities, they all testified that she was a psychopath with narcissistic and hypersexual tendencies. The jury agreed and found her not guilty. The judge sentenced her to an indefinite period of time in a psychiatric hospital. She would be there until doctors determined that she was no longer a threat to herself and others.

Mr. Campbell told her that he would start the appeal process and advised her to be on her best behavior while he tried to get her transferred. He played it straight and warned her that should she be found sane, she would probably be retried and if she was, the death penalty would be in play, so it was in her best interest to stay 'crazy' for as long as possible.

After a few months, he finally got her transferred out of the state mental institution. Doll didn't appreciate his efforts until she spent her first month there. The accommodations, the food, the staff, everything was horrible. When he notified her that she would be transferring to Blackstone, she was so grateful she could

have blown him on the spot, but again, she held back. This was the first time she hadn't used sex to get what she wanted and things were still working out for her. He promised to visit her as soon as he had any news regarding her case.

When she saw Blackstone, it looked more like a castle than a nuthouse. Doll imagined herself as the princess in a fairy tale until they took her to the small room that would be her home for as long as she was confined there. It looked a lot like the cell she'd just left. *So much for being on my best behavior.*

She quickly got used to their daily routine. Up at seven, medication, breakfast at eight, followed by either time with a psychiatrist or in the day room depending on the day of the week, lunch at noon, medication, exercise and then crafts. They ate supper at six, back to her room by seven and then another dose of medication before bedtime. The schedule never deviated and the only high point of her day was the medication. It gave her a mellow buzz and kept her calm. Needless to say, boredom crept in and she started looking for something to keep her amused. Being in the day room gave Doll time to check out the other patients. Most of them didn't warrant her attention, but one day after lunch, she saw an attendant walking with a woman who looked slightly familiar to her, although Doll couldn't quite place from where. She tried to get closer, hoping to overhear her name or anything that would give her an idea of who she might be. Everyone treated this woman as if she was fragile and an attendant always stayed near her to prevent any interaction with the other patients. Doll wondered why she had been institutionalized. Hell, she killed six people and no one guarded her. Whose safety was the attendant concerned with, hers or the other

patients?

Terri was so far back into the daily routine of Blackstone Hospital that, sometimes, except for being with Jay, she didn't remember leaving. Every night before she dozed off, thoughts of him would give her a momentary warm feeling of contentment and satisfaction. She always slept soundly. That feeling promptly vanished every morning as once again she became aware of the harsh fluorescent lights and her hunger. She would look around surprised to find herself back in her hospital room. When all her memories came flooding back; how Shevaughn had stolen her child, her return to Blackstone and her botched suicide...the sound of the alarm used to alert the staff after the night nurse came in and found her unconscious, the attendants rushing her to Blackstone's emergency room and having her stomach pumped...her waking up the next morning, somehow knowing Jay would never come to her again because she had failed and her punishment meant losing him forever. That hurt the most.

Each day the realization struck her with a feeling of defeat and hopelessness so strong it made her physically ill. Her womb ached with the knowledge of what would never be. If she thought her life had been empty before, she really didn't have a clue of how lonely it could be, until now. Terri's stomach cramped and she doubled over, her arms tightly crossed as if trying to hold in the pain. She attempted to stand and found her legs were too weak. She began to sob uncontrollably. The sound alerted Nurse Harry, an attendant who came in to check on her. After the night they revived Terri in the emergency room, every morning for the last four years always started exactly the same.

Nurse Harry placed Terri's morning medication directly into her mouth. Since the staff discovered she liked to palm her medication, they had all been instructed to make sure she swallowed all three pills. The nurse ran a latex-gloved finger around the inside of her mouth and under her tongue. Terri never fought or attempted to bite her. You had to care to fight.

Satisfied that she swallowed her meds, Nurse Harry helped Terri get into the shower. While she stood under the hot water washing, the attendant stripped the cot and found the large urine spot. Every night, Terri would take off the adult diaper and wet the bed. The attendant believed she did it just to make her angry.

After changing the bed and helping her dress, she led Terri to the cafeteria for lunch. Each day Terri woke up later and later. Nurse Harry knew that was another sign of severe depression, escaping through sleep. But instead of forcing her to get up on schedule, they let her make her own rules. Terri would stroll in and sit at the corner of the long lunch table alone and wait for Nurse Harry to bring her the meal. As much as hospital administration warned staff about not getting personal with patients, the attendants wondered if Terri would ever really come out of it and start interacting with others. If not, they feared she was doomed to live in the land of psychotics forever.

Everyday she watched the woman shuffle into the cafeteria for her meals. Always silent, Doll wondered if she could talk. Then, out of the blue, she heard the woman scream.

"You don't know me. How dare you address me by my first name? It's Mrs. Becker to you! Say it...Mrs. Becker. How many times do I have to tell you?"

So, Mrs. Becker is definitely not a mute and she has an attitude problem!

When Mr. Campbell paid his monthly visit, she asked him to do all he could to find out about her fellow patient, pretending she was worried for her safety. She didn't mind the wait. After all, it wasn't as if she had somewhere to go. He returned the following month and informed her that Mrs. Becker had been married to the infamous Eric Becker and had also lived with Jacques Diamante before his suicide. Doll realized what the two had in common and when she heard that, years later, the Becker woman had tried to kidnap the detective's daughter, she hoped she had found an ally. *Everything happens for a reason.*

Both had lost people they cared about because of Detective Shevaughn Robinson-Williams, *or whatever the hell she's calling herself these days.* She learned all about Detective Robinson when she was in her "true crime" phase in Juvie. Doll had read everything she could find on the "Ace of Hearts" and "Black Jack" case.

The next time the two of them were within speaking distance, Doll moved as close to her as she could without Nurse Harry stepping in. She made it a point to politely introduce herself.

"Well hello, Mrs. Becker. My name is Dahlia Henderson, but everyone calls me 'Doll'. Detective Williams put me in here, too. That kinda makes us like family, doesn't it?"

Terri stopped and looked at the tiny girl in front of her.

"What did you say?"

"That I'm here because of Detective Williams, but you know her so well you probably call her Shevaughn, huh?"

Terri grabbed Doll's shoulders and stood so close that when she talked, Doll felt a fine mist of saliva on her face. It smelled of toothpaste and vitamins.

"Don't say her name. Don't you ever mention that bitch to me again if you know what's good for you."

Right then, Doll got her answer. If she ever wanted to plot on getting even with the know-it-all cop, she had a partner in crime in here with her. She stepped even closer to Terri and lowered her voice to make sure Nurse Harry didn't hear her next words.

"Well, that's gonna be a little hard to do if we want the bitch to suffer. You do want her to suffer, don't you? If so, her name's bound to come up eventually."

Terri looked at the petite woman-child, afraid. *How did this little stranger know what she was thinking?* "Get away from me, you little demon," she whispered. "Stay away from me and stop stealing my thoughts."

"It's only because I feel the same way you do," Doll whispered back. "She just stood there when they shot down my Reuben."

"Are you saying she got your man killed?"

"Yeah, she was there and did nothing while he died."

"She's done it to me twice." Terri turned to her attendant and spoke politely. Her voice sounded younger than her years. "Would you mind if I talk to my new friend by myself?"

Because this was the first time Terri interacted with anyone other than staff and although Nurse Harry couldn't hear what they were saying, she couldn't deny the positive effect it seemed to have on Terri. She decided it couldn't do much harm and made a conscious note to check the newer patient's files to see if there were any reasons to keep them separated.

"If you need me, I'll be right over there at the desk," Nurse Harry informed Terri before she sat down no more than eight feet away. The two patients could now continue their conversation without worrying about being overheard.

"Someone's got to stop her and we sure can't do it from in here. At least one of us needs to be on the outside. I'm probably going to be here a long time and if I ever do get out, it'll probably be to go to prison. Now you on the other hand, once they say you're sane, you'll probably get time served and be free to do whatever you please."

"Yes and I could come visit you whenever I don't know what to do next."

"Yeah, you could. From now on, I need you to listen to me and do whatever the doctors ask so you can get out of here. Together, I know we can do this. She thinks she's through with us, but she's sadly mistaken. Are you with me?"

Yes, indeedy, I certainly am. It felt good to finally have somebody on her side. She was now part of a team and Terri felt confident that between the two of them, revenge couldn't be far behind. That night was the first time in a

long time that Terri went to bed actually feeling more in control than she had in years. When someone has a goal and a purpose, everything seems to fall into place. She couldn't wait to see what they would cook up for Detective Robinson.

The next morning, Terri woke and forgot about her usual crying. She watched as Nurse Harry checked her bed. The sheets were dry. Feeling stronger and more independent than she'd felt in years, she went into the shower without any help.

Turning on the water, she relaxed under the hot spray, but she turned it off when she thought she heard a man's voice.

"Jay?"

She heard a nasty snicker that gave her a chill in the steam-filled bathroom. And then he spoke. Terri recognized the voice and it filled her with a terror she thought she'd long forgotten. She felt the slightly cooler urine trickle down the inside of her left leg. *Why would he come back now?*

...Because he can...

"Sorry, bitch, he can't make it. Looks like you're stuck with me."

Full House

Prologue

Bethany Peters sat in the oversized rocking chair by the window and surveyed the completed nursery. A large woman with breasts that almost hung to her navel once she removed her bra, she stood a formidable five foot ten, close to 200 pounds. In her younger days, men thought of her as voluptuous and compared her to Jayne Mansfield, but age and gravity had taken its toll.

She was feeling pretty satisfied with herself since now all she had to do was wait on her boys to do as they were told. She'd given birth to five good-looking boys, although each reminded her of her husband in a different way. Ardon, Belial, known as Lyle to everyone except his mother, Caleb, Darius and Ethan were such obedient sons. They would do whatever they could to keep her happy.

Her relationship with her boys was so unlike the one she'd had with her mother. Her mother had been a hard woman to please...or love. One day, she sat Bethany down and explained her views on life. She got the impression she would always place second when it came to her own mother's affection.

"The man comes first," her mother affirmed. "We're here to make things as easy for him as possible since he's the reason we have such a nice house, clothes on our backs and food in our tummies." Bethany reached the conclusion that the only reason her mother gave birth to her was to substitute for the maid they couldn't afford.

As the oldest of three, it became her responsibility to make sure her brother got ready for school. Every day, she would get up, wash, get dressed and put her robe over her school clothes, then go and wake her brother. As he showered, she made his bed and breakfast. Her sister, the youngest of the three, was still in her mother's care, but Bethany knew all that would change as soon as the little one became school age.

She always remembered the one morning when everything went wrong; her brother fought getting up, she burned the Wheatena and later when she arrived at school and removed her coat, she looked down and saw she still had on her pink, quilted robe. Her classmates thought it was hilarious and the news of her faux pas spread faster than chicken pox in a preschool. When she got home and tried to explain the humiliation to her mother, the woman quickly brushed it off.

"It's no big deal, Bethany. A year from now who will remember? You need to get over yourself."

That very day, Bethany vowed she would never confide in that woman again. She promised that she would have more compassion for her children and she made good on that promise. After everyone thought her husband left her for some floozy he met in their congregation, she devoted herself to her boys. However, in reality, the couple never left at all. They were both buried deep in the back of her

flower garden, fertilizer for her beautiful prize hollyhocks.

One cold winter evening, she'd thrown a dozen garden-grown castor beans that she allowed to flower and seed into his chili and watched him collapse hours later from the stomach pains. The ever-attentive wife, she cared for him as he suffered through   the gut-wrenching vomiting and blood-laced diarrhea for three days until he finally convulsed and died. Then a couple of nights later, his fool mistress had the nerve to come looking for him when he didn't meet up with her as promised. God's house was full of women who prayed for a man and didn't care if he already belonged to someone else.

Bethany had been ready for bed, yet she invited her in and offered the woman a seat at her kitchen table.

"It looks like he left both of us. I'm thinking it's no great loss, he's probably found our replacement. Good riddance to bad rubbish, I always say. I think it's time for us to celebrate. Would you care for a drink? I know I could use one. How 'bout I make you a Chivas and soda?" Before the woman could answer, she left her sitting at the kitchen table and went to get the liquor.

She didn't mind helping the Lord bestow a little vengeance. When she returned empty-handed from the buffet in the dining room where she stored her alcohol, Bethany crept up behind the woman and using the belt from her robe, strangled her, thus making sure her husband and his little harlot both got exactly what they deserved.

Once alone, she raised her five sons with an iron fist and never let another man get close enough to hurt her again. A man would never be her number one priority. And it was all worth it because her sons repaid her with unquestioning

loyalty. There wasn't anything they wouldn't do for their Mama. Ardon, the eldest, took over as head of the family. He left high school and took a boring job at a local clothing factory. For his reward, Bethany placed him in his father's place at the head of the table and Ardon accepted the responsibility. He even helped her keep the younger four in check. That wasn't the only placed he filled in. She taught them all that the most important commandment had to be honoring thy mother.

Bethany slowly got up and ignored the popping sound her knees made as she walked over to one of the five cribs and ran her long, pale, unusually thin fingers along the smooth whitewashed wood railings she'd had her sons sand and paint together under her watchful eye. Soon, they would grant her wish. Smiling, her attention was diverted by the sound of the peeling, weathered red cellar door closing. They were finally home.

♥♦♣♠

Their first shopping trip to a crack house scared them almost as much as what might happen if they disappointed Mama. She could give you a look that made you sick with guilt. Not to mention the brutal punishments her mind came up with.

It was after one a.m. and with the new moon, the night was darker than black. They'd been let out of the car two blocks down from the intended target with instructions to be back in an hour with the girl. The two blocks felt more like two miles. As they passed the dilapidated apartments and dirty lots filled with enough garbage to resemble a city dump, the men huddled closer together, gathering strength in each other's presence. They could see their breath join into one cold, white cloud.

When they got to the address, they looked at each other in disbelief. It definitely looked like the worst house on the block. The stucco exterior, decayed in several spots, revealed glimpses of the wood frame underneath. Several windows were bricked up and the ones that weren't were broken. A freezing wind swept by, going straight through their coats. It was less than thirty degrees outside that February night. Remnants of snow and ice littered the three front steps. Holding the shaky banister, they carefully stepped around the ice patches and opened the peeling, unlocked front door. Once in, the smell of depravity and dilapidation mixed with urine caused their stomachs to lurch. They walked past what looked like a young kid sitting at the front of the hallway. A slowly swinging, bare sixty watt light bulb hung from the ceiling on a frayed cord, revealing his presence and the trash and dirt that surrounded him. Shocked by the skeletal impression of his face, they split up to go around him and to cover more ground in less time, Ardon going right and Belial going left. After not finding who they needed on the first floor, they met and went up the next flight of stairs together, stepping around people leaning on the banister or over the ones who sat on the steps with their heads held down.

In the last room on the second floor, they found her. She sat gazing out of a broken window and they couldn't tell if she was high or just daydreaming when she didn't react to them entering the room. Ardon stood behind her while Belial sat on the windowsill and faced her.

"Hey, are you alright?" He looked into her eyes and saw that her pupils were so dilated it was hard to tell their color. She was flying. "How would you like to make fifty dollars?" Belial continued. "That's twenty-five each for me and my brother. That should help you for a while." The girl

nodded "yes" and smiled. She was still almost beautiful. "But you have to come outside to our car. It's warmer in there than in this dump."

Belial and the woman stood up and Ardon placed her between them. She slid her arms through theirs like a daisy chain and the three of them left the building together, no muss, no fuss.

They walked a block and were crossing the street before she spoke up.

"Hey, where's your car?"

As soon as they stepped up on the curb and Ardon saw their car coming towards them, he surprised her with a knockout punch to her jaw and she immediately went limp with a quiet gasp. The brothers easily carried her between them, their bodies shielding her from anyone sober enough to notice that something might be wrong. The car door opened and Caleb waited with rope and a clean strip of cloth in hand. Between the three of them, they swiftly bound and gagged her.

No one spoke during the long ride home. As they left the city, the girl came to and this time they used the spray bottle Mama had prepared and given them with the instructions to spray it up her nose should she become difficult. They didn't know what it was or how Mama got it, all they knew was that it worked like a charm. She was so out of it, Belial pulled up her blouse and bra and they took turns sucking her breasts. Belial allowed Ardon to go first, out of respect, patiently waiting his turn. They noticed that, even unconscious, her nipples became erect.

When they pulled up to the well-maintained farmhouse on the outer edge of suburbia, the three young men carried the girl around back. It was as if they didn't have to keep

up the pretense of a normal family and the decay their lives evolved into showed in the back including the remnants of last summer's flower garden.

They ignored the swamp-like backyard as they went down the steps to their underground room. Although the front of the home definitely had curb appeal with its red with white trim façade and manicured lawn, the back of the house, due to the lack of nearby neighbors, had been neglected. It wasn't easy because she came to again and she had a lot of fight left in her. She thrashed around as she fought against her restraints, but when she saw the size of the blade Caleb showed her, her eyes widened and she'd become a lot less feisty and a lot more afraid. Belial and Caleb held her while Ardon unlocked the cellar door. They carried her into the large padded room they had all worked on together, like a family project.

There were five small cots, bought from an army surplus store, lined up in a row with their headboards against the one concrete wall that wasn't padded. Each bed had a pair of handcuffs attached to both sides of the head and foot boards. There were no pictures on the concrete walls, no TV, no phone.

They laid the girl on the fifth cot in the back of the room and closed the cuffs around her hands and feet and rattled them to make sure they were secure. Before they left, they each kissed her on her lips without removing her gag and glanced back at the girl lying spread-eagled on the cot before shutting and locking the heavy cellar door.

They were relieved that the hardest part was now over and eagerly anticipated what would happen next. The three were on their way to get their Mama when they heard her slow footsteps coming to get a closer look at their

catch of the day. They ceremoniously opened the cellar door and presented her to their mother, looking like the male equivalent of Barker's Beauties. A young cocoa complexioned woman in her mid-twenties stared back at them with frightened eyes.

"Nice," Mama said as she walked around the bed, surveying her prize. The girl was a tad thin, but with a shower and a meal she'd be quite attractive. She was no more than five feet five with large dark brown eyes and hair that looked like it hadn't seen water in weeks. Finally, Mama could show off her corn-rolling skills.

"I'm gonna take the gag off, but only if you promise to be quiet and answer my questions. Any screaming, I'll leave and let them do whatever they please", she said nodding in her son's direction. You understand?"

The girl nodded and one of the men stepped forward to remove the gag.

"What's your name?"

"Tarah."

"How long have you been a crack whore?"

"I'm not."

"Not what, on crack or a whore?"

"I ain't no ho."

"Okay, honey, how long have you been using?"

"About six months."

"And how do you support your habit?"

"I…"

"You sell your body, just like Mary Magdalene. That

means you're a whore, dear."

The girl didn't argue and hung her head.

"We're going to give you chance at a clean life, help you change. You do want to change, don't you?"

The girl nodded affirmatively.

"Speak up, dear. Do you want your life to change?"

"Yes."

"That's yes, Mama."

"Yes, Mama"

"Good girl."

Mama turned to her sons.

"Bring Tarah upstairs to the bathroom." Ardon unlocked the handcuffs, easily carried her upstairs and left her alone in the bathroom with Mama.

After Bethany shampooed her hair and gave her a hot bath, Tarah turned out to be much prettier than Mama first thought. Her cocoa skin had only a few imperfections. They'd gotten her in time.

A toothbrush and lotion were on the fake marble beige bathroom counter and plain white cotton extra-large T-shirt lay across the closed toilet seat. Bethany instructed her and watched as Tarah brushed her teeth, rubbed the vanilla-scented lotion all over her face and body and put on the oversized shirt. When she finished, Bethany sat on the commode, instructed Tarah to sit on the floor between her legs and braided her hair. The whole process took less than two hours.

"Don't we look nice? You know, you remind me of a picture I once saw of Saint Josephine Bakhita. Did you

know she was a Black saint?"

Mama didn't wait for an answer and changed subjects. "I'm afraid you're going to have some discomfort from the withdrawal, dear, but I have something that will help." She shook out five capsules.

"They're harmless, I promise." Bethany opened her hand and touched each pill before placing them in Tarah's hand. "This is a multivitamin and this is vitamin C. The last three are herbal. This one's called Saint John's Wort", she said pointing to the smallest, light brown capsule, "and this white capsule is valerian." That pill was actually a combination of schisandra, a Chinese herb Bethany believed had properties that increased sexual desire and valerian which acted as a sedative, but she neglected to mention the combo. "It'll help with the cramps and this is skullcap," she finished, pointing to the yellow one. All her herbal ingredients were from her garden. She carefully hand packed the capsules herself, months ago.

"They'll make it easier for you. Take them," Bethany commanded as she ran the tap and filled the bathroom tumbler with cool water.

The girl took the glass and did as she was told, swallowing them all.

"Now I want you to get some rest. We'll bring you some food in a bit."

Around 5 a.m., Ardon came back down to the cellar with breakfast; eggs, sausage and buttered toast. He also brought an apple and a cup of tea, but she nodded her head negatively and refused to eat any of it. He placed everything on top of the metal trunk that sat near the bed and served as a night stand. Ardon sat down on the bed beside her. He touched her tightly braided hair and

caressed her cheek.

"Tarah, right?" He spoke softly as his hands brushed across her nipples.

"Yes."

It was a good omen that she too had a biblical name.

"Well, Tarah, you've been chosen." Ardon hands gently trailed from her breasts to past her navel. He reached down and ran his finger up her exposed womanhood and quickly brought it to his lips. He closed his eyes as he sucked and savored the taste.

"Not only did we get you off the streets, but we're going to take care of you and help rid you of your addiction. You will be blessed with redemption. It's going to be easy. All you have to do is obey."

He put his moist finger deep between her legs and although he could feel her resistance at first, Ardon didn't stop until he brought her to a shuddering climax. When it ended, he fed her some of the eggs and toast. Even though the eggs were cold, this time she accepted the food. He left her without saying another word and locked the door behind him.

♥♦♣♠

You had to be a fool not to know that no one would look for the women they were choosing. Crack houses were their new supermarket. Of course, you had to pick through a few to weed out the ones who were already shriveled by the drug and look for the ones that were soft, yet firm to the touch, like fruit. And if they were Black, it was a shoo-in. It didn't take a rocket scientist to know that the search would be short, if any at all and her family would remain safe.

Besides, there wasn't a prejudice bone in her body. She really didn't care what color her granddaughters turned out to be. Bethany thought most bi-racial babies were beautiful. Ever notice how you could take two of the ugliest people, one Black, one White and somehow the combination seemed to bring out the best features of the two? And with her boys' looks, the odds were stacked on their side. As long as they accomplished what she wanted, no…needed, she really didn't care at all.

She stood in her bedroom and looked at her sons, sitting lined up on her bed, all showered and anxious. They were ready to begin.

"I want to do this in reverse order, so Ethan, the youngest and most virile, we'll start with you, tomorrow it'll be Darius and so on."

She saw the disappointment in her three older son's eyes, yet out of respect they remained silent. "Don't worry, you'll get your turn," she said sternly. "Ethan, come with me."

Bethany led her son to the cellar and spoke before she unlocked the door.

"You need to remember the main reason the Lord gave us sex is procreation. Your purpose is to make a baby. No sicko stuff, do you understand? You have one hour and then I'll come back and let you out."

♥♦♣♠

As soon as he heard the click of the lock, Ethan quickly got busy and tried to recreate every perverse sex scene he'd ever witnessed in the porno magazines and tapes his older brothers provided. He removed the gag and replaced it with his throbbing manhood, warning her to be gentle.

During the first forty-five minutes he found out that, with the leeway the handcuffs gave them, he could get her into almost any position he wanted. Ethan savagely raped and sodomized her until he heard the key in the lock and then quickly switched as he made sure they were in the missionary position, exactly the way Mama wanted.

CPSIA information can be obtained at www.ICGtesting.com
Printed in the USA
LVOW041226140112

263895LV00002B/2/P